T0113389

BULLETPROOF GIRL

Also by Quinn Dalton

High Strung

BULLETPROOF GIRL

STORIES

Quinn Dalton

WASHINGTON SQUARE PRESS
New York   London   Toronto   Sydney

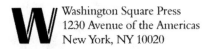
W Washington Square Press
1230 Avenue of the Americas
New York, NY 10020

Some versions of the stories in this collection have appeared in the following publication: "Endurance Tests" in *Emrys Journal,* Spring 1995; "Back on Earth" in *Pearl* Magazine, winner of 2001 annual fiction contest; "Dinner at Josette's" in *StoryQuarterly,* Winter 2001; "Midnight Bowling" in *Glimmer Train,* Spring 2003; "Graceland" in *Ink* magazine, May 2004; "Package" in *Emrys Journal,* Spring 2001; "Dough" in the *Baltimore Review,* Spring 2003; "Lennie Remembers the Angels" in the *Kenyon Review,* Spring 2003; "Shed This Life" in *ACM,* Summer 2002; "How to Clean Your Apartment" in *Cottonwood,* Spring 2001.

ISBN: 0-7434-7055-9
ISBN: 978-0-7434-7055-1

First Washington Square Press trade paperback edition April 2005

10 9 8 7 6 5 4 3 2 1

WASHINGTON SQUARE PRESS and colophon are
registered trademarks of Simon & Schuster, Inc.

Interior book design by Davina Mock

Manufactured in the United States of America

For information regarding special discounts for bulk purchases,
please contact Simon & Schuster Special Sales at 1-800-456-6798
or business@simonandschuster.com.

For David and Avery

Acknowledgments

I thank the fine literary magazines where these stories appeared originally. Also, I'm grateful to Nat Sobel, Greer Hendricks, and my husband, David, always.

Contents

BULLETPROOF GIRL

Endurance Tests

Two days after his dog gets hit by a car, my son starts playing dead. I'm washing dishes when I see him through the kitchen window: sprawled in the backyard, neck bent in a tight angle against the bottom of a tree, the undersides of his arms mushroom pale. I run for the back door, plates rattling on the counter, my sudsy hands slipping on the knob. "Chris!" I yell, on my knees next to him. "Chris!" Crying as I reach to straighten his arms and legs, lift his head from the hollow of the tree root. But I force myself not to touch, not to damage him further. "Please," I whisper.

Arms wobbling, I push myself to my feet to call 911, and then I see him smile. Just slightly, the corner of his mouth tucking into the cheek. Squinting up at me through one slitted eye. "Gotcha."

Behind the bushes, at the back of our yard, was where I'd dug Jake's grave. It was dark as I shoveled pieces of wet earth and piled them to one side, and I wasn't sure how well the shrubs would camouflage. But Chris had already seen the heavy garbage bag dragged behind the garage and the towel, rusty with blood and dirt, stuffed into the bin. I'd said it would be better to stay in his room, knowing even as the words pressed past my lips that he wouldn't. His face against the front window, watching me pass. Me slapping the mound with the shovel, knowing it wouldn't matter how flat it was; he wouldn't forget what he had seen or turn his mind from what was gone.

The next night, my ears twitch as Chris fizzes motor sounds in the bath, varying them for each boat, each speed. My breath loud in my ears at any silence.

"Hey, Mom," he calls. "Can you get me a towel?"

I jump from my bed at his voice, try for nonchalance in mine. "I thought second graders remembered that kind of thing," I say from the bathroom doorway.

"Come on, Mom."

"Just going with what you've told me." The phone rings, and I point a finger at him. "No splashing all over the floor."

Wet head flipping water with the nod, a fierce motor sound. *I'm busy here.*

Back down the hallway, I grab the phone just before the answering machine clicks. "Hello?"

Silence. "Oh, sorry, I almost hung up."

Ben. "Hi," I say, no nonchalance this time, just a compression, a loss of air.

"I thought you weren't there."

"Chris is in the bath."

"Well, that's what I was calling about."

"His bath?" I joke hollowly. Faint motor sounds buzzing down the hallway.

"Come on, Elise. Chris. When I should pick him up Friday."

I can't get used to visitation rights. Sometimes, I want to shake Ben at the front door and make him explain why he's so good about getting his two weekends a month, when four years ago he couldn't wait to leave us both. Other times I feel sorry for him. On the good days.

"And why aren't we doing Saturday like normal?" I flip through my desk calendar, phone cord twisting around my wrist.

"Because I want to take him up to the cottage. I told you last time." He had, but I want to make him tell me again. This is my game. Playing amnesia.

"Are you sure he's up to being away from home two nights in a row?" I bargain.

"Elise, he wants to go, and you know it."

"So it's just going to be you two?"

"Of course."

"Guys' weekend, huh?"

"We might look for a dog. I know he misses Jake."

"No dogs for a while unless you keep it," I say, and he sighs. I've won this round, but it doesn't matter. My ears twitch again, scanning for splash sounds, but there are none.

"All right, whatever. When can I come by?"

"Six. See you." I'm already hanging up, his good-bye tiny and canned. I glide down the hall, remembering playing Indian when I was Chris's age, silently moving over leaves. I'm on patrol, ready to catch him at it this time.

I push open the door, and he's face down, arms and legs splayed, hair clouding out from his scalp.

"Chris," I demand. Then shout. I look for a heartbeat to tremble the surface, but then I can't wait; I'm on my knees, sliding on tiles, dragging him from the water, maybe more roughly than necessary. He twists, reflexively throwing his arms around me, sucking in air. But his eyes are still closed, as if that alone can maintain the illusion.

I sit him on the mat and lean against the tub next to him,

not caring that the water's soaking through to my underwear. "Why are you doing this?" I watch him breathe, touch dripping horns of hair, try to replace my grab with gentleness.

No response. Even now, shivering, arms wrapping around his chest, he doesn't open his eyes. He grits his teeth to stop their chattering.

"It scares me when you play dead. Is that what you want?"

He opens his eyes and hugs himself tighter. "I want my towel."

That night, I stare at the ceiling for a good hour before finally giving up on sleep. Downstairs I'm looking through bills. Too late to call Marcie, my closest friend, even with her late hours and the time difference.

In our small town, Marcie was the only child whose parents were divorced. Her father had moved out to the Midwest and remarried. My father was gone, too; dead of a heart attack only two years after I was born. So Marcie and I were linked, daughters without fathers, and our mothers let us wander between our houses like sisters.

But it was the summer of the endurance tests that glazed our friendship, preserving it for later years. The drills started by the creek that ran behind all of the houses on our street. The first test involved walking barefoot over the sharp stones that washed down from the quarry. Sandals for markers. That first day, Marcie moved them farther and farther apart as the sun angled down through the trees, and I wouldn't back down, even when the wrinkled skin between my toes bled. We limped home. Then at it again, the next day. It was Marcie who pushed me to get up when I crouched, soaking my raw toes in the trickling water, our secret preparation.

In bed again, I set my own marker in the gravel. There

won't be any discussion about playing dead. Something tells me there might be better choices, that I should be patient and communicative, *talk through the problem,* all the wisdoms I might offer a parent complaining of a homework-refusing child on teacher conference night. But in times of discomfort, we turn to what we know, and my accountant mother wasn't one to *facilitate self-esteem* through *family involvement* after a full day of crunching numbers, for which she was paid far less than her male counterparts. So the next night, I'm all business, helping Chris pick out school clothes and making him a lunch downstairs while he selects a story to read to me. But when I come back upstairs, he's already turned out the overhead light; only the night light glows beside his bed. Stretched on his back, eyes pinched closed, chin pointing up in an angle defying the relaxation of sleep.

I sit on the bed, my hip against his rib cage, and run my fingers through his fine brown hair. His father's hair, exactly. "Chris," I whisper in his ear, letting my lips tickle him. "You aren't fooling me. OK?" This is too much; he squirms and opens his eyes.

"Mom," he moans, stretching the word into two syllables, "I was sleeping."

"No, you weren't." I match the singsong in his voice.

"Yes, I was."

"Honey, please. Give me a break."

"No!" Angry now, he twists away from me, shoulders curled into his neck.

Much as I had done, those nights of fiercely whispered arguments, to Ben.

Marcie and I were writing and occasionally visiting in college when I met Ben. I was new to dating, on which Marcie alternately teased and coached me. During fall break of my senior year, I spent a weekend with her at Amherst, where she was studying political science on scholarship and secretly dating her married professor. When I told her Ben and I were going to get married when I graduated, she shook her head. "With all the men I've dated, you'd think someone would've asked me by now." Books and notes surrounded her on the narrow kitchen table. She rolled a tube of lipstick under one hand. "Not," she said, "that I would say yes."

That spring, my mother flew with me to Ohio, where Ben's large family lived. She walked me down the aisle of the small church; Marcie was my maid of honor. The reception took place on Ben's family's farm—sweet wine and slices of roast beef on sun-dappled paper plates. I would have agreed to live there, if he had suggested it. But we came to this town because Ben and a college friend planned to start their own architectural firm.

Ben wanted to design a house for us, but there was never time between my teaching and his fledgling business. We bought this house, and I was happy that it was near the elementary school and that it had a big front yard, which I imagined crowded with our future children and their neighborhood friends. Over the next six years, Ben knocked in walls, moved doorways, and added skylights and porches and landscaping, as if these would make him believe we weren't living in a row of houses as uniform as beads on a string. When I wanted to discuss children, offering to quit my job, Ben said we couldn't afford it; what with a mortgage and the firm's uncertain future, we needed my teacher's salary. I knew exactly what he was trying to do when he brought Jake home from the pound; he wanted to put me off, substitute a dog for a child.

Of course, once Ben had agreed to fatherhood, he seemed to embrace it, but somehow I felt his meticulous preparations were more for himself than our child. He built a crib with high slats; he installed an intercom system—the speaker on my side of the bed. He spent long hours working at the growing firm; we needed a safety net, he said one night, pulling a pillow to himself. Instead of me.

Eating dinner Friday evening, I study Chris as he checks the bright-green watch his father gave him with the same upward snap of his wrist. He glances at me, as if he feels guilty to want to know the time. His duffel bag waits by the front door. "Are you excited?" I ask.

"Yeah. Dad says he's going to take me out in his boat."

"That sounds good."

"And he's gonna let me ride with him on his jet ski."

"Would you like some more milk?" I'm at the fridge without waiting for Chris's answer, imagining him in all that water, all those cold waves.

"Dad said he knows a man who has beagles, and he might get me one."

"How about you let Santa bring you one."

"But Christmas is far away!"

"Did you do your math homework?"

"Yes, but—"

"Did you pack your toothbrush?" I ask, although I'd watched him drop it into his red bag.

He doesn't bother to answer; he knows this is my way of derailing him. Playing distracted. Instead, he gets up to help me clear the dishes. He's unfailingly polite on the weekends he goes with his father, as if to make it up to me for leaving. It doesn't help, even though I appreciate the gesture. I already feel rattled and lonely, anticipating the time without him. The first couple of years after the divorce, I got dressed up when Ben came because I wanted him to think I had suddenly developed a full social life. I knew it was ridiculous. I felt like those soap opera actresses Marcie and I despised, waiting for our cartoons to begin. We sneered at the rich women answering phones in silk dresses, sleeping in red lipstick. *How fake,* we said. We didn't know adults ever needed to pretend. So I hated how I couldn't help myself at first. Playing desirable. These days I don't bother to dress for those few minutes at the front door.

Doorbell, two short rings. Efficient. I let Chris get it. Ben steps in, and I take my time coming to greet him. He's still tan from the summer, started a beard. Button-down shirt open at the throat, a sweater loose across his shoulders. He catches Chris in his arms and bends to pick up his bag.

"Have a good time," I say. Smiling like he's someone I'm passing on the street.

"Thanks," Ben says. And then, "OK, give Mom a kiss."

I lean in for it, closing my eyes so as not to face Ben that closely. Then I shut the door behind them and hold on to the knob, not wanting to walk through the empty house, touch what Chris has left behind.

Saturday night: video rentals and lesson plans. I give up and call Marcie, tell her about the playing dead.

"I don't know either," she says. "I don't even know how to get along with Phillip's kids!"

"I can't even talk to him about it. I couldn't say, 'Don't,'" I tell her, "'do this with your father,' because I don't want to give him ideas." I'm looking out the kitchen window, the backyard tree where Chris folded himself yellowed with porch light. How long did he wait for me to notice?

"Did you tell Ben about it?" Refrigerator door opening, a cork pulled from a bottle. I pictured the sound bouncing against high ceilings, paintings.

"No. He'd have ten ways I should have handled it. And I can already see him deciding all Chris needs is a new dog," I say, yawning. The thought exhausts me. "Such a problem solver. But I'd be the one training the thing and cleaning up after it."

And then there's what I really feared about telling Ben: Chris playing dead in the white lake waves—only not playing dead but drowning—and Ben lulled by my explanations. Playing tough.

But Marcie has moved on to Chicago's latest snowstorm and the competition for her job in the prosecutor's office. She's living only a couple of hours away from her father but refuses contact with him. Says he had his chance. Me pouring a glass of wine I don't need, wanting to say the same to Ben. Trying to imagine her life in that lake city, her apartment in some tall, narrow building, her freedom to choose her future, as Ben chose his. We hang up, and I think of the years gone, the tests by the creek, the day she pushed her curly hair behind her ears and then pulled mine into a rubber band; she never stopped talking, never gave me a chance to object. A lawyer even then. "We don't have any choice but to be strong," she'd said. Words flattened by the rubber band held in her teeth. "You know? We have to stick together."

I didn't know. Not then. I closed my eyes and tilted back my head as she pulled the ends of my ponytail to tighten the band. "This stuff could come in handy," Marcie continued.

"You never know when you'll have to give it all you got." She clenched her fists, and I knew she meant it.

We kneeled on a large, flat stone beside a deeper point in the creek. Between our two pairs of hands sat the watch Marcie had just gotten for her eleventh birthday—narrow, orange-gold, made for a small wrist. "OK, I'm gonna count to three and then dunk." I felt my heart speed up as she counted; my breaths caught higher in my throat. "Go!" she said and then gulped in air as she plunged her face into the water. Me watching from the corner of my eye as I did the same, skin slapped by the stinging cold. Hands sliding down the side of the rock, digging into smaller, rounded stones in the creek bed. Holding ground. I imagined my face becoming stone, the blood rushing to my head and freezing there. But I did not want to be the first one up. I dug farther into the silt, bit my lip, squeezed my eyes shut tighter. Then I half heard, half felt Marcie pull up to breathe. I followed, and we collapsed on our backs, gasping and coughing. Water running into my ears like cold tears.

Marcie checked her watch. When she could speak, she sat up. "A minute and three seconds," she said, after she caught her breath. "Now, let's try for a minute fifteen." On our knees again. While we were under, she grabbed my hand, and we twisted our fingers together. When she started to rise, I held her for one last moment so we could come up together.

Sunday evening, Ben at the door with Chris over his shoulder, asleep. "Could I get some coffee before I hit the road?" he asks.

"Sure." Heading for the kitchen, wondering if he had questions for me. *Any idea why Chris pretended to fall out of the boat?* Playing the better parent.

"It's OK; I'll make it," Ben says, following me. Chris awake now, reaching for me in a way that makes me pull in my breath in gratitude. Ben hands him over. I help him upstairs, into pajamas, into bed. Downstairs, Ben's opening cabinets, lost in the silverware drawer. I wait until the coffee maker finishes gurgling before I come back. Ben is in the living room, looking out the front window, although in the dark all he can see is his own reflection. Tips the mug back, almost finished. Holds the liquid in his mouth as if he can't bear to let it in, a habit I recognize.

"So, was it a good time?"

Ben swallows, nods. "I think I completely wore him out."

"Well, I guess that's good," I say. He looks at me, then inspects his mug, and I can't find anything in his expression as he takes it to the kitchen.

"I have to get going," he says. I'm at the door, waiting to open it until he's close enough, so as not to appear too eager. Playing polite. He breathes a good-bye, barely looking at me as he passes, hunting the keys in his pocket.

Next day, Chris and I are heading home from school, the backseat loaded with his backpack and my students' geography tests. Mondays are art days for the second graders, and in his lap Chris cradles something wrapped in a brown paper towel.

"What is it?" I ask.

Chris pulls back a corner of the coarse paper, allows me a peek. "I made it last week, but we had to let 'em dry."

"Did you start anything new today?"

"No, I painted it today."

"What is it?"

"Wait until we get home," he orders, and I laugh, knowing this is payback for all the times I've made him wait to open fast-food, grocery-store trinkets.

"So, was the lake fun?" My hand on his arm as we turn a corner. Wanting to press him against the seat, hold him safe. Every time.

"Yeah. We went out in the boat a lot."

"Sounds like fun."

"Yeah," Chris says, but he lets his head fall back against the seat.

"But?"

"Well, he didn't let me drive."

Good for you, Ben, I think. We pull into the driveway; I wait while Chris lifts the garage door. It takes all his strength, but he can do it, insists on it. We carry our respective bundles inside. I can't hold back my question. "You didn't give your dad any scares this weekend, did you?"

Chris pulls his bag and art project closer to his chest. "I told him we're gonna wait for a while to get a dog."

"OK." But I'm not satisfied. I drop the keys, the papers in my arms threatening avalanche. Chris sets down his bag, picks up the keys, unlocks the door. Faces me for a moment before stepping back to let me in. "It's easier when I'm away," he says. "When I'm here, there's everything. You know?" Doesn't wait for a response, which is good because I don't have one. Except: *You think I don't remember everything, too?*

But I keep it to myself, watch him unwrap his creation on the kitchen table. A red and blue lump. Red for him and blue for me—he told me these were our colors once. "Why red?" I had asked. "Because it goes with blue," he said.

I lean to hug him, breathe in the bubble-gum scent of his Ninja Turtle shampoo. "It's beautiful. Where do you want to put it?" The colors blend as I turn it.

"Watch out, it's still a little wet."

He's right. Smudges on my fingertips. I put it down. "The mantel?"

"No. It's for Jake."

I try to add up what he means. But he's ahead of me. "I want to put it on his grave." Holding the back door open with his foot.

"OK," I say, pretending to have known what he meant all along. Playing smart. Wondering how many times I've missed the point. I pull a mason jar from a cabinet. "Let's put it in this so the paint doesn't get messed up."

Chris slides the lump gently through the mouth of the jar, his hand still small enough to set it gently on the bottom. I follow him through the yard, past the tree, through the bushes to the mound. He squats beside it, digs a shallow pit with his fingers, places the jar in it. Pats the dirt back around it to make sure it won't fall.

Tonight Chris's light is off when I come upstairs from packing his lunch. He's on his side with his back to me, and I lean against the door frame, weighing whether to come in. He rolls over and squints at me. "Can I have a back rub?"

"Sure." He flips on his stomach, and I give him the Chris version of a back rub—long, gentle strokes from his shoulders to the base of his spine. We don't speak. When his arms relax and his cheek sinks against the pillow, I slowly swing my legs onto the bed, prop myself on one elbow, pull his body into the curve of mine. I hold him close, as I did the day Jake was hit.

It was wet—that was the driver's excuse. Chris and I were getting ready to take Jake for a walk. Streams of rain on the windowpanes still thinning, and Chris tying his shoes while Jake circled and sneezed with excitement. I grabbed a light jacket and called out for Chris to do the same, but he was chasing Jake outside. At the open front door, I bent to pick up the leash and my beat-up loafers, watching Chris rearing back to toss a bone treat to Jake. Jake knew this game; he was already backing up, preparing for a long chase.

"Good throw!" I said, the bone sailing high into the air. Jake lost track of it but kept running full speed toward the edge of the yard. And then the silver-blue car rounded the curve. I think Chris and I realized at the same time what was going to happen, but he had a head start on me as he took off down the driveway. I dropped the leash and my shoes and jumped off the steps onto the grass, fear already so heavy in me I thought my knees would buckle. In two running strides, I was on the driveway, and I don't remember if what I heard were the squealing wheels or my own screams to Chris as my feet smacked against cement. I don't think I have ever seen anything move so fast as my own son, running toward that car. But I caught him—tackled him, actually—and pressed his face into my neck as Jake was thrown from under the front wheels.

The man got out of his car as I hurried Chris inside, ushering him upstairs. "I'm so sorry," the man said. He said it again. He looked truly dismayed, brown raincoat frowning with wrinkles. Did I speak to him? To the garage and back outside with an old towel and garbage bag; maybe the man said nothing and just watched me cross the street to collect the body, eyes narrowed so as not to see clearly how the skull had been crushed.

That night, holding Chris until his eyes closed in tear-swollen sleep, I wanted to call Marcie, but it was late. If I had called, I would have said that she had been right all along about the tests, how we had to be strong. But I would have told her those creek days were pale preparation, that we never could have held our breath long enough or set our shoes far enough apart.

Back on Earth

It happened fast and slow. When she thinks of it, she sees a series of frozen images, no movement, but struck with light and dark. Like a slide show. The man had climbed onto her balcony and pried open her living-room sliding-glass door with a crowbar. He woke her almost gently, shaking her shoulder, then showed her the gun, the small black tightness of the metal, and pressed it to her head. He made her roll onto her belly and laughed at her for wearing only a T-shirt and no underwear. "Wantin' it," he said. She knows he said other things, but these are the only two words she actually remembers.

She called her mother after 911, and as the sirens boomeranged closer, she felt as if she had been flung into space, spit out by the Earth, left to orbit the moon.

For the first week afterward, she does not leave her mother's house except to look at mug shots at the police station and go to the doctor. The mug shots are digital; she looks at them on a computer. The X rays the doctor insists on show the haze of her bones, and she is surprised by their anonymity—they could belong to anyone.

Her boss says to take as long as she needs. Her brother comes from Chicago to help her mother move her things out of the apartment. What doesn't fit in her mother's house goes into climate-controlled storage. She wishes she could crawl into a box, too, pack herself away. The person she was before no longer seems to fit in any room, in any conversation. She tries to pinpoint the moment her old self left and decides it happened sometime between when the man strolled down her hallway like a nonchalant guest and when she finally felt able to slide from her bed onto the floor and crawl to the phone. Actually, she had dragged herself, legs heavy and bloodless, like in nightmares when she tried to run and ended up lurching forward on her knees. It was as if the electricity in her muscles had simply gone out, leaving her in a permanent dream, her speech clogged in her throat. Only the structure and casing were left, the skin and blood and bones, the parts with enough mass to be photographed, enough instinct to survive.

At her mother's house, she watches television in the cathedral-ceilinged great room. She walks barefoot on the sea-green carpet, follows the sun across the peach walls. Her mother pulls her blonde hair back in a headband rather than curling it, takes off the first week to be with her, drive her to the doctor or the police, feed her, and—she knows this—make sure she doesn't kill herself. The medicine cabinet empty except for toothpaste and hairpins. Not even aspirin. But she has no intention of killing herself. She has no intentions at all.

After her mother goes back to work, she falls into a schedule. She drinks coffee until her mother leaves, then checks all the locks, pulls a knife from the kitchen rack, and balances it on the side of the tub while she showers. If she can manage it, she gets fully undressed. Except for the underwear. The cotton-Lycra blend that comes to her waist, normally reserved for periods. Sometimes she can't take them off, even for the shower, so she just exchanges the wet ones for dry ones afterward.

Then she puts the knife back and watches cable until her mother comes home for lunch. One day on CNN, there's a story on the international space station. A team of two Americans and two Russians are breaking the record for the longest time spent in space by humans. They are repairing and updating the station and conducting experiments. They are in fact one of the experiments. They give each other physicals every day and measure muscle mass to track atrophy. They exercise to keep from getting too weak for Earth gravity. The video image, gray and bulging with distortion, shows the Americans and the Russians eating and drinking together, wearing T-shirts and running shorts, doing slow somersaults and hamming for the camera.

The next afternoon, there is a follow-up story on how the astronauts receive supplies. Russian and American ground control send a small ship called *Progress*. The ship is launched to reach the station's coordinates, but it's up to the Russian cosmonaut Sasha to jostle the station with thrusters so *Progress* will dock softly and exactly. If *Progress* misses, they might not be able to get back into position, and it might take weeks to get new supplies.

She watches the small, black tubular ship dock on the station. It moves as if falling through water. One of the Americans, Dell, says it will take two or three weeks to unload *Progress* of its oxygen canisters and dried beef and water and toilet paper, and then they will load up *Progress* with their waste and send it back, where it will disintegrate in Earth's atmosphere. Never to be seen again, Dell says, pressing his fingertips together and then quickly spreading them, to show what he means. Dark eyes behind thick brows and a white plane of cheekbone. Lips the same gray-white as his skin. There is very little color up there.

That night, she thinks of how satisfying it would be to slowly unpack each weightless item, to float from one small compartment to the next, the blue glow of the Earth on her skin as she passed each porthole. She imagines herself doing this the way she once imagined furnishing a house for herself like the one her Barbies lived in. She had fallen asleep night after night planning the pink elevator, the white shag rugs, and satin curtains. Before she falls asleep, she thinks of Dell, the way his fingers pressed together and parted, the gentleness of the gesture.

The next day, her AIDS test comes back clean. Her mother listens to the message on the answering machine and cries. She sits down at the dining-room table and rests her head on her arms. "Thank God, thank God," she says. Then, recovering, "Were you out when they called?"

She shakes her head. "I just didn't want to answer the phone." She strokes her mother's arm. Her friends are starting to call the house now that her number at the apartment has been disconnected. A man she went out with a couple of times called, too. Justin. A good name. She thinks of his glossy black hair, his ocean-blue cotton shirts, the golden-orange ring of his voice. He moves in her mind like an old home movie, bright and shaky and distant. She liked him, but she will not call him.

The next weekend, her brother comes again from Chicago to visit. He tries to get her to go out to dinner with him. "Just the two of us," he says, out of the corner of his mouth, trying to sound conspiratorial, as in, *Let's get away from Mom, like we used to.* But she knows he's already asked their mother if it's OK that they go out alone. She's always been close with her brother, once his translator and protector as a child when his speech impediment made him a target of teachers and bullies alike. She remembers carrying him, his warm weight on her chest. Now, she knows he wants to comfort her the way she did so many times for him, but she can't accept it.

"For what?" she says, not asks. There's nothing out there. She imagines the front walk and the prickly Florida grass crumbling at the edges to empty space. Milky Way where the curb would be. Blackness and stars and silence.

The night before her brother flies back to Chicago, she hears him talking quietly with her mother in the living room. She's never noticed how much he sounds like their father. And when she thinks this, the next thought pulls the air from her lungs: *I'm so glad he died before this happened.* In college she'd had a miscarriage—she had not even known she was pregnant and mistook the contractions for cramps. Her parents came to the emergency room, and she remembers the skin of her father's face looked as thin and delicate as paper, as if it would tear if he spoke or breathed.

In the paper the next morning, she reads of another rape, similar to hers. This makes three times where the attacker used a crowbar to enter an apartment. There was one rape where a woman was assaulted in her car, but the description she gave of the man was similar to other descriptions, so they are counting that one, too. They refer to the man as the crowbar rapist.

She takes a deep breath, decides to skip the shower. She was not able to give a very good description of the rapist. For example, she could not remember if he was dark skinned or light, tall or short, if he wore a mask or not. The other women say he was white with a medium build. She tries to remember him that way but cannot. He could have been anyone.

She thinks about calling her mother, asking her to come home for the day, but decides not to. On CNN, the astronauts are having a party. A new team is replacing the Russian cosmonauts. The going-away party is a few days early because another shipment is due in the next day, and then there won't be time. The video shows Vassily opening a small jar of caviar. "To celebrate!" he says in heavily accented English. He toasts the camera. Blue-white face, sawdust-colored hair floats around his ears. Dell slices a lemon into sections and passes it around. The other American says, "Cheers!" He toasts the camera, too. Dell touches his lemon slice to his nose and inhales. He presses the palm of his hand to his chest. "It grabs at your heart to smell something of the Earth," he says, his eyes staring through the camera, like a man who's seen his own death.

She gets up from the couch and finds a lemon in the refrigerator. She slices it with her shower knife and presses a section to her nose. It smells just cold at first, but when she squeezes some of the juice out, the scent escapes. She can feel it in her eyes.

She takes the lemon slices with her to the bathroom and draws a hot bath. She drops the slices in the water. She takes off her sweats and underwear, even though the cool air against her buttocks makes her want to cry. She steps into the water and submerges herself completely except for her knees. Her arms float by her sides. She opens her eyes to the stinging heat and looks at the blue tinge of the water on her ribs, the way small bubbles rest on her belly and wobble slowly to the surface where the lemon slices float. She pictures her life outside this water, this house, and tries to think about going back to it but gets hung up in the details. Where would she find the iron? Where are her keys? Who would she talk to and what would she say?

A few days later, hunting the astronauts, she finds only a concerned-looking, glossy-lipped reporter filling the screen: "According to high-level sources at NASA, the American supply ship known as *Progress* collided with the Mir station early this morning, knocking it out of orbit and severely endangering the lives of the crew. Ground control and the crew are trying to stabilize systems on the aging station, while also determining what course of events led to this emergency . . ."

She clutches the remote, unable to move. Mir is a mosquito hovering over the skin of the planet. When she closes her eyes, she is in the apartment, and it is dark, green streetlight glinting off the gun barrel. She did not cry during the rape. She believed at the time that she was calm, and she remembered trying to keep the gun in view at all times. But she couldn't see it toward the end because the man was holding her head down in the pillow. When he came, she tried to lift her head, but he wouldn't let her, and she was convinced that he was going to kill her. And then she was thinking, not really in words, but in an urge, like for food or air, *I can't die with this man inside me.*

But she didn't die. He had left her to remember, like the other women. Now CNN had video of the *Progress* ship bumping into the station. A bump, like a moth hitting a screen, then a full flip, then a coming to rest. It looks so slow and unreal she can't tell whether it's a computer re-creation or just the weird scale of the planet swell in the background. She thinks, *I am on that planet, somewhere, sitting here. And so is he, and the crowbar, and the leftovers of everything we've done and been.*

Late that night, unable to sleep, she turns on the TV to find Dell talking. It's just his voice with b-roll of the space station orbiting the earth and replays of *Progress* crashing, but she recognizes his voice. He says they are repairing systems one by one, and now that they have sealed the oxygen leaks, they are out of the worst danger.

Cut to Boris Yeltsin speaking forcefully to assembled reporters. A woman's voice translates. "Indications clearly point to human error in the accident, not systems error," he yells, pounding the table like a father angry at a son's fender bender, but his words are a mumble underneath the woman's careful English.

"Fuck you," she says to the TV. She goes to her bedroom, the room she had slept in as a girl. She opens the closet and looks at her work clothes, all pressed and hung by her mother, and tries to remember how they go together. Before, she was a public relations writer for an agency. That's how she thinks of everything now, in terms of before the rape and after. The Before person knew how these kinds of public snafus worked, be it an oil spill or a miscalculation of quarterly earnings. Apologies were made and people got fired. The people whose faces you could see, not the people who really set the policies or made the crucial bad decision. In the case of the space station, both the American and Russian teams would probably be fired for making their countries look bad. Their careers finished. The Before person knew this and accepted it.

The person she is now is missing things—a skin, pragmatism. She runs her fingers across her fitted linen shirts in ice cream colors, her tailored skirts and slacks. She thinks of the astronauts floating in their small metal womb filled with Earth light, quietly working within the body of the ship to keep their bodies alive, the ball below them boiling and clotting with people who do not care about them and will not protect them. She goes back to the living room and turns off the TV and tries to write a letter to the astronauts advising them of their best PR strategy, but she stops after one sentence: The best thing I can tell you is to decide where to go next.

Her first day back at work, the women in her office greet her warmly, concern weighing the corners of their eyes, as if she has returned from a long sickness. The men, including her boss, try to do the same, but she reads something different in their eyes, and it looks like fear.

One coworker, the one she likes least, comes into her office late that first day.

"I just wanted to offer my condolences," he says. He likes big words. *Condolences* instead of *I'm sorry.* He touches his squarely buzzed black hair as if forgetting he cannot run his fingers through it. His earring reflects light onto his cheek. Before, he used to try to undermine her work to compete with her for the best clients in the agency. He questioned her decisions to launch a release as opposed to holding a press conference, to make a client available for an interview as opposed to acting as spokesperson. He tried to make her look incompetent in strategy meetings.

She briefly considers reaching across the desk and grabbing him by his leather, zippered vest and smashing his face into her desk. It infuriates her that he would even refer to what happened to her at all, especially with any kind of sympathy, fake or real. She knows he thinks he's a good man by doing this, so enlightened. She knows what he wants is a reaction, or at least a thank you, so he can have permission to screw her later.

"Eric," she says, in the tone of a teacher calling on a student. "You offer condolences when someone dies. I am not dead. Now get the fuck out of my office."

His head snaps back as if she has thrown something at him. His skin seems to tighten against the bones of his face. She watches him turn to leave, listens to his office door close, and smiles even though her stomach hurts and her teeth are chattering.

On her way home, she stops at the Orange Tree Shopping Center and calls her mother from her cell phone to ask if she needs anything at the grocery store. She scans the parking lot before getting out of her car. It's six in the evening, early summer, sunlight still jabbing through the palm trees lining the parking lot entrance. She walks past the large plastic orange mounted over the entrance, picks up a green basket. In line, she studies the impatient, preoccupied faces of other women, most of them professionals on their way home like she is, getting dinner ingredients. She wonders if any of them have been raped. She looks at the men and wonders which of them would rape if given the chance to get away with it. A college friend of hers once said that all men were born rapists; that only socialization could tame them. At the time, she thought the idea ridiculous. "Well, then we're all potential criminals," she'd said.

She remembers feeling connected to people then, to the women who washed dishes in the college cafeteria, to the guys playing pickup basketball in the courts near her dormitory, to the bearded telephone repairmen clinging to the tops of poles while they worked. She liked to think of everyone trying to survive together on this planet, all of them needing food and water and air and sunlight, all of them facing the unknowns of the next moment.

But now she feels no obligation to smile at the cashier, a

teenaged girl working after school. The Before person would have seen herself in this green-aproned girl, working for spending money, for freedom. She remembers this but doesn't feel it anymore.

The only real connection she feels is to her mother and brother and to the astronauts, although the astronauts are easier because there is no history with them; they don't know who she was and who she is.

That night, the network news reports the American team is coming back from the space station. They have to debrief everyone on what caused the *Progress* collision. She opens the laptop she brought home from work and searches for Dell+astronaut+NASA. She finds out that Dell is from a town only twenty miles away. She looks at a map of Florida and imagines seeing it from space, the crooked finger, the limp, ragged appendage. She decides to meet Dell, to tell him she doesn't blame him for anything.

Two days later, two things happen. First, her mother calls her at work to tell her they think they've found the crowbar rapist. She sits in her office chair too fast, loses her breath momentarily. A clammy weakness spreads from her knees up to her thighs and down the backs of her legs.

"Are you there?" her mother asks.

"Yes."

"They've asked us to come in tomorrow. To look."

She hangs up and resists the temptation to slide onto the floor, under her desk. She rubs her legs, trying to bring the blood back to them. Would he have killed her if she'd screamed? As far as anyone knows, he doesn't kill. She didn't even think about screaming. She would like to do that right now but knows that she won't. There's no way to go back after something like that.

Then the second thing: On her computer screen, a news banner slides across the NASA Web site: American team on the ground . . . Click here for interview. She pushes the mouse, and the arrow staggers to the link. In streaming video, men in gray jumpsuits lift the two astronauts from the shuttle into waiting chairs. Their legs splay limp in front of them. Reporters and photographers tighten their circle around them. Dell is on the right, squinting in sunlight. Someone straps a microphone to his head.

"How do you feel?" a reporter asks.

"I'm happy to be home, to smell the air again," Dell says. He reaches slowly forward and pulls his legs together, one at a time. Still in their space suits, both men look like smiling aliens, released prisoners, their faces moon-white and hollow.

The prisoners line up in front of her, all of them gazing at the floor or the doorway, trying to look anonymous, like men who don't know anything about crowbars or guns. The fluorescent light grays their skin. One man stares right at her without seeing her: He keeps the middle finger of one hand erect the whole time, pressed against his thigh.

Her mother clutches her arm; her breathing is choppy and loud in the darkened observation room. The air tastes thick and metallic, like chewing on an eraser.

She looks a long time, as long as she can. They are all white, varying heights, eyes dark under the shelf of their foreheads. "I don't know," she says. "None of them."

"Are you sure?" one of the cops asks.

The blood is leaving her legs, so that she has to lean on the table to hold herself up. Her feet tingle. "No, I'm not," she says. "It could be any of them."

"Shit," she hears one of the cops whisper. The woman cop.

A week later, as she is getting ready for work, she sees Dell on the local morning show. He is wearing an orange golf shirt and navy pants. The colors vibrate against his pale skin.

"Are you getting used to being back on Earth?" Ned the talk-show host asks.

"I've been gone so long I'll have to find out who I am again," Dell says. He smiles and brings a cup of coffee to his lips, and she is surprised to see him move at an Earth pace, no slow dance-like sweep of the arm.

She imagines driving to the station, waiting for him in the parking lot, calling out to him as he leaves. "Dell, I just wanted to congratulate you," she would say. "You did really well up there under a lot of pressure."

He would thank her; he would want to talk more but not be sure what to say.

She'd tell him she was a reporter. "I'd like to interview you, too," she'd say. "But about what really happened up there with the crash. About how you stayed calm and did what you needed to do to survive. Because most people don't understand that, Dell. They think people get over fear like a virus; they just forget it once it's over." She would make up a name to introduce herself.

The thought makes her feel as if she might fall away from the ground.

Ned is asking Dell about his childhood, how he trained to become an astronaut, what they cook in space, what he had to give up.

"A family," Dell says. "I've never been in one place long

enough . . ." His voice fades, and there is a pause that's too long for TV. Ned clears his throat and says, "I was asking about the foods, if certain foods give you indigestion in space."

"Oh," says Dell. Then Ned asks what Dell liked best about being in space.

"Well, the stars, I guess. You know, you can actually begin to perceive the depths between them when you're outside the atmosphere . . ."

No, she thinks. She wouldn't lie to him about being a reporter. She feels he's been lied to enough, by the very people who were supposed to protect him. Instead, she would tell him that she wanted to write his life story, and this is the truth. They would meet in a café, and he would talk, and her pen would curl words across the page, paper scraping on the sugar-sprinkled table, and they would stay there until it was finished. She stretches out on the couch, drops her keys on the floor, closes her eyes, and begins to see it.

The astronaut is an affable man, so he smiles even though the studio lights make him sweat and the newscaster smells like red meat and beer, too sweet. Ned wants to know fun facts about space because that's what his audience of young professionals and retired schoolteachers from New Jersey want to hear. He's got demographics in mind. He doesn't want to know how it feels to watch the Earth rolling below you and think about dying. But the astronaut sees the best in people. He'd wanted to go into space since he was a small boy. He has the patience of someone whose dreams have come true, who has gotten to the other side and found it the same. He leans forward, and his seat squawks under his weight.

"But I'm not going to be an astronaut anymore," he says.

"Why not?"

"The ship is old. It should be retired with dignity. I used to feel safe there, but this time I could feel the space pressing in on all sides. The others felt it, too. Like it was taking over our bodies. Every time a system went down, we died a little bit."

The astronaut looks past the studio lights, through the metal ceiling and the blue rim of sky, until he feels the moon-light again, milky white on his face.

"When the *Progress* was coming toward us, I saw its black shiny skin, and it felt like a menace. I felt it would swallow us."

The astronaut can smell his own body in the heat rising from his skin, the salt smell of sweat, and something else, like dust, like rocks. He remembers the party for Sasha and Vassily, the day before the collision, the way the lemon slices made him think of his mother, how she used to put them in her bath, the oil sheen pink and aquamarine on the water, and sometimes she would let him get in with her when he was still quite small, and he could feel the lift of her breasts against his back, the brush of her pubic hair against his buttocks, and she would wash him and let him stay in the water even after she got out, and he would close his eyes and float and think: *This is how it will be in space.*

The astronaut sees his home now, an empty condo in a ring of identical white condos around a bowl of a golf course. They glow purple at night like moons. "I think I'm just getting used to living on Earth again," he hears himself saying. Only he's no longer in the studio. He's standing next to water, the swimming pool near his house. A woman takes his hand. It's night, a spill of stars in the northeastern sky, each predicting the next one's fall.

"Me, too," she says, turning to him. She has the calm face of one who has considered death. She tosses a handful of lemon slices into the water and removes her jacket, then her sandals. The oily scent of lemons rises from the water. She seems terrified, but she keeps moving, slowly pulling the pins from her hair. The astronaut looks at the water and then back at her. He bends to untie his sneakers and peel off his socks.

They step into the water, their clothes lifting around them. They hold onto each other as they slip under the surface of the water. She opens her mouth and lets the water rush in, press against the back of her throat. The astronaut holds onto her tightly, trembling, and he may be crying, but he isn't sure. The lemon slices glisten like lights in the silence above them, like stars that will tell them where to go next.

Dinner at Josette's

She and Malcolm had broken up, she said, and true girl-friend that I was, I asked her to lunch and at lunch asked her to dinner. She touched my arm with cool, polished fingertips and said, "Oh, I could so use the company right now."

Josette was thirty-six and had talked of marrying Malcolm. I thought she was brave to end it when the nights he refused to sleep over, to make love, increased. I secretly believed him to be gay or maybe bisexual—a couple of years before I met Josette, Malcolm and I had lived in the same apartment build-ing, and I saw him often with one man. I never knew if he remembered me. Or perhaps he thought I didn't recognize him, since his look had changed—crew cut, tight T-shirts, and boots traded for shaggy hair, silk button downs, and sandals.

I called at seven. My husband was out of town, and I intended to ask Josette to meet me at the café, where we could discuss the shortcomings of men. She answered the phone in her throaty party voice; I heard pans hitting burners in the background. "Malcolm's making his special spicy meatloaf. Would you care to join us?" she asked.

Why was I surprised? Dinners were a form of expression for Josette; this one to announce that somehow the relation-ship had been restored, and I was to witness. "I don't want to barge in," I said, but there was no backing out, a slice was waiting for me.

I walked to Josette's house, admiring the brightening sliver of moon over the town houses, the sound of voices and plate clatter at the café. Josette had bought a large wreck of a house and restored it lovingly. She was on her little back porch, drink in hand; I whistled and she waved. Then I saw Malcolm in the shadows, dressed all in black, reclined as if slapped into his chair. They stood as I approached, and I felt like a boat coming to dock, unable to change direction.

"Good to see you," I said to Malcolm, and he nodded, not really looking at me. I smiled, finding his eyes, and his shoulders relaxed.

"Oh, we are out of margaritas already," breathed Josette. "Between dinner and these windows, I can't think straight," she said, gesturing toward the second floor, where in the waning light a workman struggled to install a window frame. Her eyelids fluttered at the sound. Black hair piled on her head, stray strands lifting in the evening air, she was one of the most beautiful women I had ever met and certainly the best dressed, that night in a lemon silk tunic and white linen wide-legged slacks, to eat meatloaf of all things, but of course with a man who had denied her what many men had begged her for. It was true that on the surface Josette and Malcolm had much in common. They both loved discussing the lines of things, attending dawn estate auctions, and spending weekends refinishing their obscure finds—this was in fact how they had met.

"I'll make some more," I said. Josette followed me inside. We gathered limes, ice, tequila. I knew my way around her kitchen, having made many meals there with her when we were both single and waiting for something in the small cluster of clubs downtown, before I married and she began with

Malcolm a relationship, as she had once described it, built on the aesthetics of sex: the most beautiful ways to have it, the most elegant rooms to have it in, on the finest antiques, the glossiest wood. She once said truly beautiful sex would have to involve more than two people, preferably several men sprawled on the high bed, ready, a muscled backdrop for the woman's smoother lines.

The meatloaf glistened under Malcolm's gentle basting, while Josette twisted limes on a porcelain juicer, liquid jetting between her fingers. There was a crash upstairs, which startled all of us. "I've got to deal with this man before he destroys my house," she said, leaving a lime half-spent on the juicer. I finished it, mixed the drinks, offered one to Malcolm.

"Actually, I'll have a martini," he said, pulling gin from the freezer. Josette's voice echoed through the ceiling; clearly there was some dispute, and when I looked at Malcolm, he just shrugged his shoulders and turned up the volume of the Latin music on the stereo.

On the porch, Malcolm lit a cigarette, offered me one, and we smoked, grateful for distraction from speaking. I had at first disliked Malcolm because he had been rude to my husband when they met at another dinner, at Josette's, of course; Malcolm had rolled his eyes when Gray said he was a computer consultant, and walked away, as if it were too boring to discuss. But later I learned that Malcolm's professional life as a landscape artist was spotty, with holes for drug rehab and depression treatment, financed by his family, and knowing this, I liked him better.

I spoke first to put him at ease. "So, are you OK?"

"Yes, I think so. I think we both are," Malcolm said. Then, after a long exhale, "How do you feel about pine bark?"

"What?"

"For the yard. There's too much shade for grass."

"Easier to take care of. I'd like a rock garden," I said, although at the time my husband and I were dreaming of a city flat with no garden and no garage, just streets and museums and places to lose ourselves among strangers. This town had gotten too tight, too familiar.

"Oh, everyone's doing those now. I designed one for this bitch on Magnolia who was so picky I finally just said, 'I don't think it will ever be good enough for you.' And walked out. I probably ate two thousand on that, but it just wasn't worth it." He sipped his martini, lime sliver twirling to the bottom.

I didn't know what to say to this, so I said nothing. In earlier years, I would have tried to continue the conversation. But marriage had mellowed me. I could sit for hours with my husband without speaking, simply enjoying our combined presence. So I waited.

"And I'm thinking about building a deck," Malcolm said after several minutes. "As much as Josette loves to entertain. It would be perfect, don't you think?"

I nodded, and then I realized he was actually asking Josette, who had come out from the kitchen just then with a young woman, who introduced herself as Amy, a new neighbor. I hadn't heard them approach over the blaring radio.

We all shook hands. I smiled broadly at her; I could feel the alcohol heating my face and chest. Malcolm brought out two more chairs, and Josette freshened our margaritas and poured one for Amy. She was young and seemed small next to Malcolm, blond hair neat behind her ears. She sat with her knees pressed together.

"So what brings you to our fine city?" Malcolm asked.

Amy was choking on her first sip of margarita; it was quite

strong, so Josette answered for her. "She came here to teach disabled children, isn't that wonderful?"

We all agreed it was.

"The only problem is the new director," Amy said. Her accent lilted; I guessed she was from somewhere in Virginia, where, as my English teacher, a native himself, had once said, people spoke as if they had marbles in their mouths. "He is a terror. This week he put out a memo threatening to fire people. I can't believe the board hired him."

Josette sat forward in her seat. She was an interpersonal skills trainer for an insurance company, and motives were among her favorite topics. She pegged the director immediately as a sociopath. "They snow you, and then, and then, people are afraid to criticize," she almost whispered, eyes wide. "It's a way to control reaction by creating action. In a past life, I was like that," she said, referring to her years in an Atlanta advertising agency where she used to make people cry, a story I had heard her tell often.

"Lots of times boards hire directors for fund-raising experience rather than personality," I suggested—I raised money for the university then. The alcohol clung to my throat; my teeth were numb.

"Did he have any gaps in his résumé?" Malcolm asked.

"I don't know." Amy shook her head, eyes watering. The drink was too strong for her, but she seemed to like it anyway. She waved vaguely at a mosquito. "I'm still new myself."

There was another crash upstairs, and Josette shot to her feet, steadying herself on Malcolm's shoulder. Malcolm took her hand, looking up at her with a concerned scowl. "Shit! That dumbass hick," she growled.

Amy stood, too, her drink only half empty, but clearly she'd had too much. "I should go."

"Oh no, no," Josette and Malcolm said together. "Stay," Josette said.

Run, I thought. *Get out of here.*

"Meatloaf's almost done," Malcolm said, but this didn't appear to encourage her.

"No, I really should," Amy said, her voice trailing. I took her drink, walked her to the front door. A Victorian coatrack seemed to scare her; she shrank from its brass hooks.

"Welcome to the neighborhood," I said. I hugged her, and she was perhaps five years younger than I, but I felt as if I were hugging a child. I watched her until she made it down the steps, then shut the door gently behind her.

I heard Josette coming downstairs and waited for her. "This house has fifty-six windows, and he wants to ruin every last one," she said. Her cheeks and willowy neck were flushed. I found a pack of cigarettes on the mother-of-pearl inlaid music stand and handed one to her. She had come a long way to get to this house. I had been to her childhood home, where her mother still lived, a cramped, two-bedroom shotgun affair on a busy road in a neighborhood recently swallowed by Raleigh's Research Triangle Park. Josette held the cigarette between manicured fingers and blew out, her forehead smoothing. She didn't appear to notice that Amy had gone. "Ah, my glass is empty," she said, and so we refilled on our way back to the porch.

We found Malcolm with his keys in his hand. "Where are you going?" Josette asked, her words stretched, slow. On the street, the window repairman slammed his truck door and drove away, a bit fast, I thought.

"Home to take a quick shower before we eat."

Josette said nothing, but I knew her very well and Malcolm well enough, and I knew the way whole conversations pass in a glance, a gesture. At that point, she was asking him to stay, to use her tiled shower and Egyptian cotton towels, to make it feel as if they were really together, even if only for a night. And he was fidgeting, saying no with his hands deep in his pockets. He left, and then Josette and I set to serious drinking.

She slammed the half-empty bottle of tequila on the porch railing, followed by two shot glasses, a lime, a salt shaker, and a knife. She poured the shots, stabbed out two lime slices, and handed me a ragged wedge and a glass. I sipped and she licked salt from her hand and tossed, pressing a wedge into her teeth, her fine, pale skin flushing deeper. I was amazed at how young she looked at that moment, as hard as she ran herself, the five-city training seminars and dinner parties and drinking and smoking, her clothes always pressed, nails and hair shining.

"So we're back together. Innit great?" she said. Eyes closed, head turning slowly from side to side, as if she heard music somewhere. The radio had been turned off. I hadn't noticed. "Same old shit."

I was thoroughly, irretrievably drunk by then. I could smell the meatloaf carbonizing on the burner, and the thought of eating it nearly made me sick. I wanted to leave, but didn't think I could walk. So I told Josette about Malcolm and the man in my old apartment building, and the night I saw Malcolm through the gaps in the stairs wearing a blond wig—jeans, tank top, and the wig and bare feet—leaning against the wall in the hallway. It was late, and the other man was there, and I had just remembered this—how had I forgotten? The man's hand on his belt, pulling.

"Stop it! Stop it!" Josette screamed, her voice tearing into the air, echoing.

I waited. I felt a surge of a fascination for Josette that was something like love but not quite. We had shared so much. We met through a mutual friend, a man who had asked us both out, first Josette, then me, as it would often happen until I met Gray. Our first evening together, Josette served homemade vanilla ice cream in crystal goblets and read my tarot cards. She told me I would be married within the year, which was almost true, and then she told me of how she had once been stalked by a married millionaire. On the night I told her Gray and I were getting married, she threw an artichoke leaf at me, her face shocked in anger, then, catching herself, a smile. At the engagement party she threw for us, the night Malcolm rolled his eyes at Gray and stalked away, she also invited a man named Nate and took him to her room after dessert, and everyone, Malcolm included, knew they were having sex. They emerged, bodies loose and throwing heat, the performance for the evening.

The sex had been a message to me that I could never have anything without something being taken away. To call her on this would have been absurd because it was a fact, she could not ever blame herself for anything.

"He's a liar; he really is," Josette was saying. "I didn't give him credit."

Malcolm's car pulled to the curb. We sat and smoked our cigarettes and waited for him to emerge, clean and ready for us.

Midnight Bowling

It was Mr. Ontero from across the street who found my father stretched out in the front yard next to his IV tree as if he'd gotten tired of waiting for someone to let him in. Lettie and Harold Bell and fat Ms. Parsons and the triplets and other people whose names I don't remember anymore stood on the lawn watching Mr. Ontero trying to save him while my mother was at work and Donny Florida and I were at school. It was a cloudy day and still pretty brisk out, typical Ohio spring; I imagine the red and blue flashes splashing the treetops on our street like the disco lights dotting the Star Lanes. Mr. Ontero checked my father's pulse and puffed into his lungs because no one else would do it. In between breaths, he told the neighbors he was an old man and had seen the Spanish flu. Everyone had said the world was ending then, which it hadn't, so he wasn't scared of any so-called plagues.

After the funeral, Mr. Ontero offered to sell back our lawn mower at the price my father had sold it to him. "Fair is fair," he said to my mother on our doorstep, tulips from his garden quivering in his outstretched hand. "No profit mongering here."

My mother slammed the door in his face. A couple of weeks later, when I started back to school, I'd see Mr. Ontero as I walked to the bus stop, bent like a question mark in his front yard, picking leaves and twigs from his silky, trimmed lawn and stuffing them into his pockets. Whenever I stopped to say hello, he told me stories about making lard soap in the Depression and earning a dollar a week on the oil rigs in Missouri City; he spoke like a typewriter, in a kind of emergency Morse code, never pausing to allow me to say "that's nice" or "good-bye" until I had to walk away or miss my bus. I'd hear his voice trail off like a plane passing overhead and feel too embarrassed to look back.

Then Donny started giving me rides to school and work whenever his car was working, and I hardly saw Mr. Ontero at all until he died last week. I rode my bike to the funeral in my pink Eatery waitress uniform, having just been fired, to say good-bye to him in his casket.

Now Donny's driving me to my college orientation, and I'm thinking about Mr. Ontero as a little boy cutting the tip of his nose off with a toy-plane propeller and having to sit still with no anaesthetic while they sewed it back on with thread, real thread, and his squinty black eyes, the last to see my father alive. His thin, reedy voice hums in my ears on and off during the two-hour drive, while my mother thinks I'm at work, saving money for our big move. The voice is saying, "You've got moxie," which he said every time I won the Junior Tournament Bowlers Association of Ohio—Rookie of the Year when I was thirteen, Bowler of the Year at fourteen, and Highest Average the next two years. My father put the trophies in the front window to signal each win. He was Joe Wycheski, the Buckeye Champion of the Ohio Bowlers League eight years running. Donny's uncle Leo, who owns the Star Lanes, puts your picture on the Hall of Fame wall if you get the Buckeye three times. My father's picture has a permanent space in a gold-speckled plastic frame.

Donny pulls into the visitor lot, singing at the top of his lungs to Led Zeppelin. A girl pulls in next to us in a red convertible and hops out; Donny doesn't notice how she crinkles her nose as if she smells exhaust from Donny's brown T-Bird with the racing stripes he painted himself—she's walking fast, bangles clinking. A gold chain gleams on her ankle.

"I'll meet you here," Donny says, and for a moment I forget why I thought this was such a good idea, going to college, where he won't be.

The first session is Campus Culture. The tour leader, a blonde woman with a pointy chin that turns white at the tip when she talks, says State has a strong gay-lesbian association, and the girl with the bangles says fags shouldn't be allowed because it runs against the Bible, which is why they're being punished with AIDS. Nobody says anything to this. Of course, now people are saying you can get AIDS from mosquitoes or saliva and that we're all being punished.

Then there are the Student Services and Learn the Library tours and a packed lunch, and at the end I'm in the parking lot waiting for a half hour with my slick gold-and-black folder, looking at this wide, green campus filled with people I don't know. I've played some lanes here, but I can't remember where they are. I watch the girl with the bangles get in her car and drive away without looking at me, even though she smacked gum in my ear for five hours. Donny strolls from behind some buildings like he's at the park, in no particular hurry. He stomps out a cigarette, unlocks my door first.

"Where were you?" I ask.

He shrugs, doesn't answer. We get on the highway again. "You know what I heard," he says. "If you can't go to college, go to State."

I roll my window all the way down, and hot air blankets us,

wisping hair out of Donny's thin, rubber-banded ponytail. Donny hates driving with the windows down, but I like it because it feels like flying, I think, though I've never been in a plane.

"Oh, really?" I say. The road melts air at the top of the next hill; the radio announcer's drilling the record temperature and humidity. At night, planes crisscross our town, spraying the mosquitoes breeding over ponds. I turn the air-conditioning on, to compromise.

"They don't care about you," Donny says.

"You just don't want me to go."

"Whatever." Donny shoves another tape in the deck, Rush this time, singing *Exit the warrior / Today's Tom Sawyer.* Head swinging forward on the guitar and drums.

What I know is, Donny applied to State, too; didn't even type out the forms. Sent it out like it was no big deal. And didn't get accepted. We haven't talked about what he plans to do this fall, unless he goes full time at the lanes like his Uncle Leo wants. Me, I just got fired from waiting tables at the Eatery because I forgot to bring ketchup to some guy. A bottle of ketchup. I didn't know what I was going to do until Mr. Todd told me about his wife's brother who works at the College of Arts and Sciences at the university, which is weird to think about, a college inside a university. He said his wife's brother would nominate me for a scholarship, even though I've already missed all the deadlines. He called yesterday and told me to go to orientation, said he had something for me. He said there's no need to talk about it to anyone because these scholarships are for special cases. But I did tell Donny because I want him to know everything.

"I'm taking a nap, OK?" I say.

No response. I lean back and close my eyes, AC mixed

with hot outside air rolling over me in waves, music vibrating my ribs. Donny's driving because my mother finally sold my father's car, which I was using, because she says we need money for our future more than we need things. Our future, according to her, is at the Savior Missionary in Marietta. The Savior, as she refers to it, is where I can get real-life experience. "Millions are waiting for the Lord's word right here in Ohio," my mother informed me yesterday. For two thousand dollars, I can get into the missionary program and travel all over the country handing out flyers and visiting foster homes. She thinks I'm going to save that much from waiting tables. So I've been going to work with Donny; I wear my Eatery uniform and change in the bathroom at the lanes. Leo's paying me under the table to balance the books, says he can't see the numbers anymore.

My mother often can't see details that don't fit her "vision," or "God's plan for us," such as the fact that I've slept with Donny, which she decided not to conclude upon discovering a package of condoms in my dresser drawer while looking for my boat-neck sailor top. Or that she's wearing her seventeen-year-old daughter's clothes and dyeing her hair a lot. Or that she's exchanging love letters with a forty-year-old married man named Jake.

Yesterday I wanted to tell her there was no way I was going to Marietta, but then she said we could sell the house and get away from here together and start a new life, and her eyes were shining and her face was flushed, and I couldn't bring myself to do it. Because I want to get away, too.

My mother went to the Savior a couple of months ago for a conference, *Faith in the Eighties,* and met Jake, who actually just lives across town, except now he is a reformed Episcopalian and went to the Savior to rescue his soul. He's apparently perfect for her, except for the married part, so my mother and he write each other letters and talk about Jesus' will. They actually mail them to each other, like the apostles, you might say. I know because I've read them, locked in the bathroom pretending to take a shower, which is what I do when I need privacy. My mother believes in privacy, meaning not being naked in front of anyone unless you're married or unless you're an innocent child, which neither of us is anymore.

I steal Jake's letters from Time-Life books stacked along the wall underneath the couch. They are stacked there because she gave away our coffee table, along with most of our furniture and all of my father's things. My mother gives things away because the Bible says to. "We won't need any of this where we're going," she said the day the church van came to pick up our kitchen table and chairs. That was two weeks go. Now we eat our meals standing at the kitchen counter.

I guess my mother thinks I don't look at those books anymore, at the 1920s discoveries of Egyptian tombs and artists' renditions of the solar system. But I found the letters right away because I still like to imagine the dry desert heat, the pyramid shadows sliding over sand, ancient priests worshipping glowing planets. I've only seen one of my mother's letters, since she mails them while I'm pretending to be at work. The one I found in a stack of bills and long-distance Bible study offers wasn't what I expected. While Jake talks philosophy, she talked plans—What do houses cost in Marietta? She wanted to know.

After I read the letters, I take off my clothes and stand on the toilet with the water running, inspecting myself in the mirror until it's too steamy to see. I don't know what I'm looking for. Sometimes I try to imagine what Donny sees when we're doing it, how I look from above, or bending over him, or from behind, when I can get him to do it that way.

My mother says I am one of the cleanest people she knows. She says it like she knows something is up. She has started threatening to make me pay the water bill. After I read the letters, I put them back between the exact pages of the exact books where I found them.

Donny rolls up the automatic windows, and I turn my head and sigh, still pretending to be asleep, and for a second it feels like we're in space, every sound wrapped in silence, and then I really do fall asleep. Then we're slowing down, sunlight sliding orange on my eyelids. Donny puts the car in park, and I hear the seat squeak as he leans across to kiss me. I want to turn away because I am annoyed with him for reasons I can't explain. But I know it will hurt him, especially after he took me all the way to State and back, so I let him think he's waking me with a kiss. Snow White. I watch him through the blur of my eyelashes. He always closes his eyes, which I don't like. I open my eyes and stick my tongue all the way into his mouth, and then I start laughing. He pulls back, surprised, then comes at me, head down, trying to lick my face. He slides his hand up my T-shirt and pinches a nipple through my bra. I sit up and grab his hands and then I see my mother's car in the driveway, a surprise. Also there's Jake's minivan with the matching car seats in back. I thought they were volunteering at the Terrace Spirit senior citizens' picnic all day.

"I gotta go in," I say, reaching for the door handle. He manages to lick my nose before he lets me go. I wipe my face with my T-shirt and leave my orientation folder on the seat.

These days our house smells of bleach. My mother carries a spray bottle of cleanser around and washes her hands whenever she thinks of it, which is often. I find her in the living room, flipping through the *Greater Marietta City Guide*. Jake's on the deck, drinking a can of pop and smoking. He keeps cases of pop in the minivan, now that he's sober. He wears khakis and knit golf shirts with athletic shoes all the time. He doesn't know I'm here, or he'd be coming in to give me one of his tight hugs and ask me what I've been praying for.

Deliverance, I'd like to tell him.

On the walls are plastic-framed religious paintings, the kind you can buy mail order in three easy payments. They don't quite cover the pale rectangles where my father's pastels used to hang—a historical study of duck and candle pins, lightning over a lake, a pregnant woman in a sheer nightgown standing at a window—all given away. The woman was my mother, but her face was turned away, so no one would know. But my mother didn't think it was "appropriate" anymore. She has told me she won't give away any of my stuff because that's up to me: I have to find my own place in God's plan. Still, I worry. There are things I don't want to lose, like my AMF Angle bowling ball and my father's shirts, which are Buckeye beige with "Wycheski" sewn in maroon cursive on the sleeve and shirt pocket.

I lean over her shoulder, moving slowly so as not to catch Jake's attention, which isn't easy since a lot of things I do seem to get his attention, like when I sunbathe or wear miniskirts, but he drags on the cigarette, squints into the backyard, oblivious. My mother's hair is pink in the sunlight; she doesn't look up. She's wearing one of my halter tops and my favorite chino shorts. Now, when I find her looking through my closet, she explains it's because she's given away too much and has nothing to wear. She studies a page in the *Greater Marietta City Guide*, glossed lips pursed, penciled eyebrows a frowned line. There is a photograph of gleaming white Victorian houses on the river. Advertisements for complexes like Eagle's Crest and Indian Falls. There are sparkling pools and workout rooms, happy blonde families strolling from their concrete patios to their minivans. My mother drives an old Buick. The spy car, as my father used to call it. Neither of us is blonde, at least not right now.

"Aren't these places built on Indian burial grounds or something?" I ask her and immediately regret it. Jake hears me; he bear-slaps the sliding-glass door open and lumbers in, grinning at me, neck muscles straining the collar of his Polo. "Tess! The Lord be with you!"

"Hi, Jake."

Jake moves in for the hug. He's blunt and square, an ex-football player, impossible to get around. I think of squeezing behind the couch, but I know this is not an option, so I just hold my breath and let him wrap one meaty arm around my shoulders and the other around my waist so my hips jam forward and my nose presses into the hairy V of his collarbone. Behind me, I hear my mother snap another page. She misses a lot.

"How's business?" I ask when he lets me go. Jake sells disaster insurance, which is odd since he believes the world is ending, and how do you insure for that? In the meantime, he talks about God like He's some cosmic weatherman or the neighborhood fortune-teller, always ready with free advice.

"Glorious!" Jake says, smiling as if he might break into song. "Your mother and I were thinking you should have your own policy."

I look at my mother and she looks at me, smiling distract-edly. I sit down next to her, angling for a better view of the *Greater Marietta City Guide*. "I'm not kidding about the Indians, Mom. Isn't it bad luck to build on consecrated ground?" I point out. Also, the river gave people malaria. I learned this in Mr. Todd's American history class. I also took journalism with him, which was my college-prep elective last year, and he says I could be a good reporter because I call it like I see it.

"There's no such thing as luck," my mother says, ruffling her fingers, mixing my words into the air. "How was the Eatery?" she wants to know, glancing at the absence of my uniform and then turning back to the Dogwood Estates.

I bend to inspect the mosquito bites on my ankles. "The bugs are terrible," I say, scratching. My mother makes a face and stands up. She brings back a bottle of peroxide and a paper towel from the kitchen.

"Listen, honey," Jake says, landing next to me. The cushions sag in his direction, pulling me to him like the black holes in the Time-Life books. I concentrate on not crossing my arms. "About the insurance."

"What, are you going to knock me off, Jake?" I smile at him and touch my upper lip with the tip of my tongue, enjoying how his eyes focus on it. He is gathering himself for a response; I can see a thought working up his brain stem, but my mother beats him to it.

"Where were you all day?" she asks, pushing the paper towels and peroxide into my hands. The latest letter from Jake advises her not to get angry at me if I'm FLIPPANT, to act NON-CHALANT because it stumps REBELLIOUS TEENAGERS. Jake writes in all block letters, underlining for effect. Mr. Todd says never to underline. He says it's a sign of immaturity.

"I was with Donny, Mom," I say. I dab peroxide on my bites, which my mom heard on the evening news will kill the AIDS virus in the event it is carried by mosquitoes. I watch it fizz on my reddened skin and wonder if my mother has slept with Jake.

My mother looks out the window, where everything is still and washed out, like an overexposed photograph. "I'm talking to a realtor tomorrow," she says, folding her arms and turning to me, pink-polished nails pressing half circles into her skin. She seems to be bracing herself. Jake watches her as she bends to hunt through her pile of church bulletins. She hands me a shiny white folder with a red-and-purple seal and *Savior Missionary* scripted in gold.

"Here you go," she says, smiling as if she just gave me a prize. From the corner of my eye, I can see Jake nodding at her. He's obviously coached her on the delivery. I take it from her and open it. Inside are several complicated-looking forms including an injury release and a Pledge Sheet with a long list of things I will agree to do and not do, such as renouncing homosexuality or using the word "Zen." There is a signature line next to a pair of floating hands pressed together in prayer. The application is titled "Foreign Missions Adventure Form."

"This is a chance for you to do something truly great," my mother says, echoing a sentence in the brochure I have just opened. My eyes fall on the words as she says them.

"Praise God," Jake says.

My mother sits on her heels on the floor in front of us, and both of them watch me read. The AC comes on and she shivers. "God has plans for us, Tessie. I really believe that. But we have to win His love. Most people can't do it."

Like your father, she means. I know this because her habit of going to church three times a week and attending conferences and seminars and subscribing to every religious booklist and newsletter she finds only started when my dad got sick a year and a half ago, first with a flu he couldn't shake, then pneumonia, then so many illnesses they couldn't be distinguished from each other anymore. He accused her of trying to make up for him and trying to make me crazy, but she didn't care what he said at that point. By then you could hardly understand him.

The memory makes my stomach feel tight and bruised. I concentrate on deep breaths, press my fingers into the Ultrasuede cushion.

Jake stands up with a grunt. "Tess, why don't you come see me tomorrow at my office," he says, closing in for another hug.

I sidestep, dropping some papers from the application. "I'm working tomorrow," I say.

Jake picks up the papers and holds them out to me, just far enough away so I have to step forward to take them. He winks when I do. "That's fine. This weekend, then," he says with his song smile. He turns to hug my mother, who doesn't seem to mind his chest hairs going up her nose. "Bless you," he says to her, as if she just sneezed.

"Bless you," she says. She walks Jake to the door, leaving me with the Savior folder and a bottle of peroxide, all the safety there is. There is some soft talking. There is perhaps a kiss. The front door shuts and locks, and my mother returns. "I'll need those forms by tomorrow," she says.

"I don't think this missionary idea is the best thing for me."

My mother motions me to the couch. I don't want to, but I sit.

"What is the best thing for you? A waitress job?" She looks at her nails and then at me. "Bowling?" She presses her lips together and waits.

I let this pass. I want to tell her about the scholarship I think I'm going to get, but I decide to wait. I saw the signature line on those forms: Parents can sign for kids under eighteen.

My silence seems to satisfy her; she stands, smoothes my

chino shorts against her thighs. Perhaps she thinks she's convinced me. Stairs squeak as she heads for her room, where, aside from the bed and a few clothes in the closet, she keeps Beta tapes with titles such as *Loving God in Pain* and *Self-Denial for Self-Fulfillment.* I notice she doesn't count the TV in our required sacrifice.

I hang my feet off the end of the couch. The AC hums; ice drops in the freezer. It's been a year since the overdose, which is how my dad actually died, not from the AIDS. That's how my mom refers to it in private, which she rarely does. As if the overdose were an event all its own, not happening to anyone in particular. Days after the doctors sent him home, my father took all of his painkillers, dragged his IV outside, and collapsed in the front yard, where Mr. Ontero found him while my mother was at work and I was in school. The coroner called it narcotic-induced cardiac arrest. Outside the family, my mother calls it a heart attack.

At the funeral, my Aunt Belinda and Uncle Percy, my mother's sister and brother who live together and take tea bags with them whenever they travel, told me that because my father was a drug addict, I would have to be more careful; I could get addicted to anything. Me standing by the hole with a velvet skirt around it and the coffin looking like it was hovering, about to blast off. Nobody said anything about the AIDS. It was easier to think about the drugs.

My dad's connection was a guy at the molding plant, where they cast the chairs for plane interiors. The police discovered this after the connection left town, and I guess he could be anywhere now, poking holes in people's skin and shooting in just the tiniest amount of his own blood, too.

Weekends, my father and I went bowling. He taught me the roll was all in the release. He was wiry with a little pot belly

I made fun of and thinning reddish-brown hair that showed
the pale skin and light-blue veins of his scalp. He wore button-
down flannel shirts tucked into jeans in the winter, button-
down cotton shirts tucked into jeans in the summer. After
years of making plane chairs, he said he would never fly
because of what he knew.

When I was twelve, he gave me the AMF Angle, the first
ever urethane make, custom teal with gold sparkles, teal being
my favorite color at the time, with my name in gold. We
watched each other in tournaments, holding our breath while
the other one glided across the floor. When we rolled for fun,
he made me discuss current events and my form and what I
could do to improve it. Mostly, though, he talked about how
good I was, and how I could do anything I wanted with an arm
like mine.

These days, when I release is when I feel my father in me
or actually, that I am my father. I feel the ball weight in my
shoulder, not the elbow joint, which is where most people
tend to hold it, and I know I look like him and that I'm feeling
the things he felt, the light strain at the collarbone, the tightening of the muscles in the back of the arm, the turn of the bones
in their sockets as the arm drops, swings back, then forward. I
imagine my muscles are his muscles, and this is how I keep
him alive.

The last time we rolled was at Rock and Bowl, which is on
Friday nights from ten to two. Donny had just gotten the
disco ball and the colored lights—he hadn't talked Leo into
the laser and the smoke machine yet. My father had the flu
for weeks by then, but he hadn't been to the doctor. The
meetings with teams of doctors and the weeks in the hospital
were ahead of us.

His hook was way off that night. "You're pulling the ball," I said. I was annoyed. Once, he pulled it five boards or more—amateur mistakes.

He ignored me. "Go," he said, as we watched three pins wobble and stay up on the second frame.

I rolled and got a strike. When you're on, you hardly feel the weight; it's just a part of you that you let go.

My father powdered his hand. "What's a perfect strike?"

I rolled my eyes. "The ball knocks down the one, three, and five pins," I said. I paused, wondering if he was going to make me recite the whole thing. He was waiting. "The five pin takes out the nine pin, the three pin takes out the six, and the six takes out the ten pin," I said. "The head pin knocks down the two, which knocks down the four and the four knocks down the seven."

"Close. The five hits the eight pin, and the ball hits the nine. You remember that," my father said without looking at me, surveying the lane. He rolled his second, shuffling forward slowly. Three pins left again. Miserable.

I won with the next roll, 168 to 132. Not a good night. "You could've done better," he said.

"So could you," I shot back.

"I'm just saying you shouldn't let your game go. You could get a scholarship, you know?"

I was going to tell him he wasn't my coach and I didn't want to hear his plans for me, but then this happened: He sat down hard in the booth as if someone had knocked his feet out from under him. I stared at him, and he gazed back at me, as if this was just a movie he was watching.

He handed me his wallet. "Go pay," he said softly. His fingers were damp and cold.

"Dad?" I said.

He made a sound in his throat and held on to the table. I

paid Leo at the bar, forcing myself not to look back at my father, not wanting Leo to see and ask me what was wrong. As I walked back to the booth, I felt strangely calm, the sounds of toppling pins muffled and distant.

My father held his arms out to me. "Help me up," he said. I leaned down to him, and he held on to my neck as I pulled him to his feet. Somehow I hadn't noticed before that I was almost his height and that he was thin, very thin. He smelled sour, like overripe fruit.

"Thanks," he said. I pulled away from him as soon as I felt him balance, and he knew it, and I could sense his eyes on me as I put on my coat. "Let's go to Harry's," he said. He patted my arm, smiling at me, waiting until I looked at him. He was breathing shallow and fast.

"I don't think so," I said. But somehow we ended up there. I remember waving to Donny in the DJ box as we left the lanes— Donny wasn't my boyfriend yet; that would be in the summer, after my father was gone and my mother had let the lawn grow to torment Mr. Ontero—and I remember I could see the sweat on my father's face, but I smiled at Donny anyway and waved to Leo, too, like there was nothing wrong.

I drove to Harry's and my father bought me a beer, which I don't even like, and Harry, who runs a tight ship, didn't say a word about it, even though he knew how old I was. My father drank while I scanned a *People* magazine, looking at the movie stars and cowboys and sick children starting foundations, and I didn't care for any of it, except for being with him in that place.

Two days later, he went to the doctor. Then he went into the hospital—full quarantine. My mother and I had to get tests. A nurse quit rather than take care of him. They couldn't handle him at Carter, so they moved him to Cleveland, where at least some of the doctors had seen AIDS before. Then they sent him home to die, and then he killed himself.

So I understand why my mother wants to move. She wants to get away from the house my father grew sick in, from Mr. Ontero's pinched eyes that watched him die in the front yard, from the town that knows our story like it's a TV special.

The voice on the Beta floats through the vents. I'm on my knees, sliding *The Solar System* from under the couch, checking for mail. My heart squeezes tighter, like it does when a roll really counts, and I'm measuring the space between me and the strike.

There's a new letter. No postmark—Jake probably hand-delivered this one right before I got home. I slip it into my shorts. "I'm gonna get ready for work," I call upstairs.

No answer as I head down the hallway to the master bedroom, where my father stayed after he came back from the hospital and where I now sleep. Sometimes I still think I can smell his cologne in the master bedroom, even though it's been more than a year. Fifteen months to be exact. Donny says he can't smell it, but I think he just doesn't like the idea of breathing Joe Wycheski's cologne after sneaking into bed with his daughter.

I fell in love with Donny's skin first and moved in from there. The day he came to the front door, he was brown with a flush underneath. He had gotten taller and full in the shoulders, his voice deeper in his chest. I hadn't seen him since school let out because I hadn't been able to go to the lanes—I wasn't ready for my father's picture on the wall with his hair slicked back and the smile he gave to people he didn't know.

It had been three months since my father had died, and Donny came to the door acting as if he'd just happened to notice the Wycheski lawn, even though it had been a wet spring and summer and his chinos were soaked to the knee. "On the side," he explained to me when he asked if he could help out with the mowing. He meant on the side from his jobs at the lanes and selling water softener and concentrated soap products to county people who have wells and brown teeth.

He came in for a glass of Vernon's and didn't look worried about breathing the air or sitting on our furniture as other people had, the few who visited after it came out why my father was sick. He borrowed his uncle Leo's tractor the first time, but after that he rolled his own push mower the three blocks and one street over to our house, and I watched him through the window or sat outside and pretended to read while he leaned on the mower, muscles moving under his skin. When he left, the air smelled like wet soil and the grass tips gleamed like a million little lights.

Then fall came, and Donny asked me to go to the Cinema Six, and later we decided that if we still loved each other by graduation, we would get married. Donny didn't mind my mother's tapes, and he said nothing when my mother started replacing my father's pastels with airbrushed pictures of Jesus walking in a crowd of children, preaching on the mount, crying on the cross.

I lock the master bathroom door, turn on the water, pull a single sheet out of the neatly slit envelope. Jake's letters are getting shorter. The first ones were three or four pages on both sides.

This one gets right to the point:

PAULA

I DREAMED I SAW JESUS FLOATING OVER THE GARAGE, AND I THINK IT MEANS WE SHOULD SKIP TOWN. MOVE ON LIKE JESUS, YOU KNOW? LIKE A ROLLING STONE.

YOU'RE MY SPIRITUAL SOUNDING BOARD, HONEY, HOW
YOU KEEP SAYING, BUT THERE'S MORE TO IT THAN THAT.
NOBODY UNDERSTANDS ME BETTER THAN YOU DO.
ANYWAY, I NEED TO SEE YOU ALONE.

LILLY'S TAKING THE TWINS TO THE LAKE THIS WEEK.
LET'S GO AWAY THIS WEEKEND AND FIGURE IT OUT. I'LL
TELL HER I'M VISITING MY MOTHER.

DON'T WORRY ABOUT TESS. THE MISSION WILL TAKE
CARE OF EVERYTHING, I'LL MAKE SURE. I'LL CALL
TOMORROW.

BLESSED BE THE LORD,

JAKE

I can see Jake scrawling in the toilet while his wife piles orange floatie wings and beach towels in the back of the minivan, the twins rolling around on the soft front lawn in matching outfits. Then I see us all together in Marietta, on top of the burial mound the Indians made, which is in the middle of town, me with a twin hanging on each hand, Jake with my mother on one side and his wife on the other. Trinities.

I slip the sheet back into the envelope. I stand in the shower, and what I want to know is, what exactly does Jake mean about the mission taking care of me?

I pull on my Eatery uniform over my still-damp skin, pink skort sticking to my thighs, and shove shorts and a halter top into my pocketbook. Through the vent, a soothing male voice says, "Think of Christ as your friend who walks with you when you push your cart down the grocery-store aisles, even when you get the paper and go to work." Music swells on the tape. Then I hear the squeak of Donny's brakes outside. "I'm going!" I call up the stairs.

No answer. I slam the door shut behind me. In the car, Donny leans across the seat to kiss me. He's redone his ponytail, nametag already attached to his blue Star Lanes shirt.

"Do you have to do that?" I ask, pointing to it.

"I'll forget it if I don't." He puts his arm across the top of my seat as he backs down the driveway. I look at the veins running in blue ropes from his wrist to the inside of his elbow, where the skin is soft and white. It looks like a man's arm, like my father's arm, and it makes me ache.

Donny's smiling. "I sold three purification systems this week," he says.

I roll my eyes. "You know they don't do anything except add salt," I say. The company has this big color brochure on how it saves plumbing from mineral buildup, but it really doesn't.

"You just can't stand it that people like this stuff."

"They like it, but they don't need it. You tell them they need it."

"You're worse than Leo," Donny says, looking at me, trees blurring behind him. I try to stare back, but I can't. I hate it when he gets mad at me. "Well, who got Leo to buy the new sound system and the laser and disco ball? Now you have to wait an hour for a lane on Friday."

"He just didn't want to go into debt."

"He's an old man, what does he know? He's still saving all his rubber bands off the paper in case there's another Depression. I guess we'll sell rubber bands then. Now, *that's* thinking."

"At least he's not a bullshitter!" I'm yelling now, my ears ringing.

"Oh, and I guess you got the corner on honesty. What about you and that scholarship deal, huh?" He slaps the wheel, shouts a laugh. "Sitting there in your uniform like you have a job."

"Asshole," I hiss.

"That's right," Donny says, voice low now, eyes steady on the road. "I'm an asshole for trying to make my own way." Smoke slides out of his nostrils.

There's nothing I can say to this, except that I want college the way I wanted Donny last fall, when the nights got cooler and he didn't need to come over as often to mow, and he crawled in the window of the room my parents used to sleep in, and we undressed under the blankets, and our skin was so warm and slick against each other that we could have been underwater.

Neither of us speaks until we get to the lanes. "I'm sorry," I finally say as he pulls into the gravel parking lot, even though I'm not sorry; I'm just tired, and I don't want to be angry. In front of us is the turquoise fan roof of the Star Lanes with the two round windows like eyes over the door. It's early yet, and there are only a few cars in front.

Donny opens the car door and stares ahead, one hand on the door handle and the other hanging down his thigh right at his crotch, the way guys do. Then he swings his legs out and slams the door behind him, walking away as if he had no one to wait for.

I lean across the seat and pop the trunk so I can get my ball. I can hear the hollow sound of the pins on the buttery wooden floor even before I open the glass doors. Then I pull the handle, and the smell of leather and beer and sweat flows out on the cool air, although bowling doesn't make you sweat unless you're nervous. It's just the smell of men who come here every Friday and never air out their shoes. It's a good smell. And a good feeling to look across the lanes, the balls coursing down the boards, through the tunnel, out of the machine, and into the hands, circulating like air, like blood.

I change into my shorts and halter top in the bathroom and take a stool at the bar. Two guys I recognize from high school are drinking draft between rolls on the end lane, my father's favorite lane. Their girlfriends, or wives maybe, both pregnant, sit in the plastic booth, smoking, flicking ashes on the floor, permed hair teased up over pale foreheads, dark circles under their eyes. Staring at the balls going back and forth.

Leo comes over when he sees me. He's wearing his favorite Beers of the World shirt with all the labels in different languages, and he's eating a bag of potato chips even though he's supposed to be on a diet. He hands me a catalog, points to a picture of a smoothie machine.

"Tessie," he says, clapping my shoulder. "You think I should order this?"

"I don't know," I mumble.

"I think it's going to be the wave of the future. You can chop up candy bars in it." Leo smacks the magazine against his thigh. "Hey, sweets, what's the problem?"

I decide not to mention the fight with Donny. "My mother wants to move to Marietta."

Leo shakes his head, strokes his mustache. He looks across the lanes to the lounge area, where the local branch of the Mafia used to entertain themselves after whacking members of the Polish contingency in Cleveland—this my father told me. Leo has never been one to ask for details. "Maybe she could go somewhere nice, like Atlantic City?" he says.

"I don't know what she's thinking, Leo," I tell him, and this is the truth.

"Could you check my math in a minute here?" Leo asks me.

"Sure thing."

"Maybe Florida?" Leo suggests as he heads to the back office.

My parents took me to Disney World on my eleventh birthday, the only time I've been out of Ohio. My dad chain-smoked and bought me foam Mickey Mouse ears and called me Minnie all day, even after I lost the ears on the Space Mountain roller coaster and cried, while my mother sat down every few feet, putting her head between her knees to keep from passing out in the heat. I used to keep a list of the best days of my life, and this was at the top. I didn't want to leave, even though I was old enough to know that there were people inside the costumes and the park closed at night. "Just leave me here," I remember saying to my father. I can still see his face tilted down to mine, almost close enough to kiss me. I thought he was as happy as I was. But now I think his expression looked something like defeat.

The sun dips behind the buildings across the street, and the white stones in the parking lot turn pale purple under the sky. More people are showing up, a couple of teams practicing for the next league event, some regulars who don't play for any team but come all the time. A shark or two scanning the talent. I find Donny at the control board in the DJ box. "Hey, can I come up?"

Donny pushes open the door without looking at me and turns back to the control panel. He's acting as serious as an astronaut, when we both know he's only got one button and a joy stick.

"Donny," I say. "Don't be mad at me."

"For what?" he asks, looking distracted. He doesn't lose his temper often, and I can tell he's embarrassed. He pulls his chair closer to the board, surveys the lanes.

I want to say for leaving you. For putting you down even

though I believe I'm right. For feeling like I see more than you can. Instead, I kneel behind him where no one can see me and press my face against the back of his neck until he turns enough to put an arm around me. We stay like that until Donny has to start the show.

It's after two when I'm helping Leo cash out in the office room—I'm doing change and he's doing bills. Donny's setting up for the next day. When we're done, Leo pats a box of napkins beside him. I sit and wait until he's finished bundling the take. His face is deep red, hairlike veins fan from his nose. He smells like cigarettes and potato chips. He takes a deep breath, slaps his thick hands on his lap. "You know, Donny's like a son to me. His parents are ghosts," he says.

I look at the floor. Leo's never talked this way to me before, like Donny's the child and we're the adults. In the whole time since I've known Donny, I've only seen his father once and his mother maybe a handful of times. They're both old; Donny has a brother and a sister who moved out ten years ago.

"You got a good head, Tess," Leo says, smoothing his gray mustache. "So I got an offer for you." I can feel his eyes on me, adding me up.

"Thank you," I say, feeling foolish.

"Year-round work, good pay, full benefits."

"Doing what?"

"What you been doing. Helping me keep the numbers straight. You got a good head, Tess. You think about it." Leo waves me away, and I get up to leave. I open my mouth to say something, but Leo lifts a hand to stop me. "I'm glad Donny's got a girl like you. That's it."

When I wake up the next morning, the house is hot and bright, and I'm alone. Upstairs, I peek in the doorway of my mother's room, and I can see the open closet, nearly empty except for her Sunday dresses and a neat line of shoes, and the TV in the corner on what used to be her bed stand, tapes stacked on the floor. I push open her door the rest of the way. Sitting in the center of her bed is a lavender duffel bag, open and waiting.

I check the coffee-table books for mail, but there's none. I shower and ride my bike to the high school, which is across the street from the cemetery, which is where my father is buried. In the hospital, when he knew before we were ready to admit it that he was going to die, he said he wanted to be cremated and scattered in Lake Erie; I remember the air in his voice, his hand on my arm, but my mother picked out the coffin and headstone as if he'd never asked for anything different. I wouldn't go there after the burial, even though I could see the marker from the school bus window every day. Now Mr. Ontero is buried there, too, his tombstone bone white.

Mr. Todd's summer-school government class is just letting out. After my father died, Mr. Todd stopped by my house every few days with homework and lecture notes, so I kept up, and after a while I could have conversations again, and then I came back to school.

Mr. Todd sees me coming down the hallway and waves. He's younger than my parents, with a son in eighth grade special ed and a fat wife with perfect creamy skin and red curly hair who always chaperones proms and wears the same cobalt-blue satin sheath dress with a black rose on one shoulder to every dance. Mr. Todd wears thick glasses and was probably a nerd in high school, but now he's a man, with sloping shoulders and beard shadow all of the time.

"Tess," he says, motioning me in. The last of the students file past us, all of them with bad cases of lecture face. He pulls a brown envelope from his desk and hands it to me. "Open it."

The letter starts with "Congratulations." I see the words "full tuition" and "special funds." There are several forms. Also a check made out to me for five hundred dollars. I bring the check, printed with an ocean scene, close to my face, studying Mr. Todd's leaning handwriting that I know so well from the margins of my papers, where he wrote, "Defend your pt. here" or "Don't leave me hanging." Ian and Leisel Todd, it says in the upper left-hand corner, above the beach scene. I look at Mr. Todd, and he smiles down at me as if I were his daughter, the way I believe my father would have smiled at me. I thank him, and he hugs me, and I hear his heart beating low in his chest, and what I feel is fear and then relief.

"Let's go to lunch," he says.

He puts my bike in the back of his station wagon. The breeze bends the envelope forward in my hand, as if pushing me along. The rectangular brick building, the gravel teacher's parking lot, the line of pines edging the practice field all look familiar but changed, flattened by my absence.

It's after three, and the restaurants in town are closed until dinner. That's the kind of town this is. Mr. Todd brought in a writer from *The New York Times* to speak to our journalism class last year, a college buddy of his, and I remember him asking where a guy could get a late-night cup of coffee around here, and we all stared back at him as if he'd asked where he could get laid.

We end up at Harry's. It's the first time I've been there since my father died. I wouldn't have gone in there if it weren't for the fact that I know I'm leaving now. I wanted to preserve his presence there, waiting for me. Mr. Todd orders, and I choose a booth in the corner, where my father and I almost never sat because you couldn't see the TV.

Mr. Todd buys a beer for himself and soda for me and two cold salami sandwiches. He sets my soda down and clinks the lip of his bottle against my can as he sits across from me.

"Thanks," I say. The backs of my thighs are sticking to the bench. I peel them up, settle them. We bite into our sandwiches. Mr. Todd drinks most of his beer in two long gulps.

"So. How do you feel?"

"Good. Nervous." The salami makes my eyes water, and Mr. Todd notices, misreads it.

"Are you OK?" he asks.

I nod. He puts his hand heavily on mine and keeps it there. "How about your mom?"

I understand he's asking whether I've told my mother or not. He knows about our empty house and about how my mom's job at the church day care doesn't pay the bills, and she was taking my tip money, which is how he came up with the scholarship in the first place. He knows enough about both of us to be my father. "She's having an affair with a married man," I answer, watching for his reaction.

He pulls his hand away, rubs his eyes. "Oh."

"She's going away with him this weekend."

"She told you?"

"No. But I know." I watch Mr. Todd pick at his beer-bottle label, and I can tell he's trying to decide whether to ask about my sources. I debate whether I'll tell him about the letters and the duffel bag, about how Jake underlines for emphasis. But Mr. Todd doesn't ask. My legs are sticking to the seat again, and I squirm to adjust.

"The forms," he finally says, tapping the envelope. "Get those turned in right away."

I nod, and we finish eating in silence. Mr. Todd swallows the last of his beer. "Tess."

I look up from the crumbs on my napkin, waiting.

"Your dad and mom." He pauses, opening his hands as if to catch the right words. "They're two extremes. You just shoot down the middle and you'll be fine."

Outside, Mr. Todd offers to take me home, but I tell him I'd rather ride. He pulls my bike out of his car. "Don't forget about me, now," he says, sounding something like my father and Donny combined.

When I get home, I hear the shower running in the master bedroom, the metallic bird-call sound in the pipes. On the radio, the announcer's talking about a cold front; there'll be record lows. The AC is dry and cold on my skin; sweat rolls down my spine. I check the coffee-table books for mail, put the scholarship envelope in my backpack at the back of the closet, and lay down on my parents' bed, listening to the water hit the floor of the bathtub.

When my mother opens the door, a cloud of steam behind her, she's startled to see me. She's got a pink towel around her middle and a white one around her head. Her face is shiny and flushed. "I was trying to figure out what you think is so great about this shower," she says.

"And?"

She shrugs. "Good water pressure. Better than upstairs. I'd forgotten." She unwinds the towel from her head and sits slowly on the edge of the bed, as if trying not to sink in too far. As the towel flops around her neck, I see she's gotten a haircut and another dye job, so all the frizzy pinkish copper is gone, and the dark, shiny hair drips in soft, water-slicked waves around her face. "What do you think?" she says, turning her head so I can see the back.

I sit up. "Are you going anywhere?"

My mother's eyes meet mine. She studies my face. "Where

would I go?" she says. Her eyes narrow, searching. Maybe she thinks she isn't really hiding anything because her plans aren't firm, the bag is not yet packed. I don't answer, and she stands, looking down at me. "How about you?" she wants to know. "Where are you going?"

"I'm going to State," I tell her. My heart is pounding. My mother opens her mouth to speak, and then the phone rings. I am nearer to it, but she reaches past me and picks up.

"Hello?" she says, turning her back to me, and I know she thinks it's Jake, hopes it's Jake. But then she turns and hands the phone to me.

"Donny," she says.

"Not the rolling stone?" I ask her, and I feel like I've jumped off a high dive. I've showed my hand now; she knows what I know. My mother looks at me, sucks in air like she's been hit in the stomach, and I know she's putting it together, all the letters unfolded and refolded, all those words reread. I swing my legs off the other side of the bed and stand up, so the bed's between us. My mother isn't moving. I put the phone to my ear. Donny's saying, "Hello? Hello?"

"Yeah."

Donny can hear something's up from the tone of my voice. "Everything OK?"

"Great," I say with exaggerated cheer. "Are you picking me up?"

"I'll be there."

I listen for the click of the phone line, put the receiver against my chest. My mother is watching me as if I'm someone entirely new to her. Her eyes are wide, almost amused. She turns and walks out of the room. Then I hear her running up the stairs.

I pull from the closet my backpack and my favorite jeans.

I also pull all four of my father's bowling shirts, which I saved before my mother cleaned out his closet. I take some T-shirts, some underwear, a notebook I didn't use up all the way from the spring. And the pictures, one of my father and me at the Buckeye tournament, one at my graduation from junior high school, one of him holding me when I was a baby, his nose to my forehead. I slip them into the scholarship envelope so they won't bend. I change into my Eatery uniform, and I put the bag back in the closet, in the corner where it can't be seen even if the folding doors are open all the way.

I hear my mother going downstairs again and then to the kitchen. My hands feel shaky, weak, as I pick up my purse and bowling ball and carry them down the hall. My mother's chopping carrots for a salad. She seems perfectly composed, her hair gleaming under the fluorescent light. She doesn't look up when I come in. She slides the carrots into the bowl and puts the mushrooms under the faucet.

"I'm going to be late tonight," I announce.

My mother slices a tomato in two. "The house goes up for sale tomorrow," she says.

I wait for her to say more, to tell me the next step. I think of hot Marietta, where the Indians buried their dead, where white apartment buildings stand like grave markers. "Why now?" I ask. I hear Donny's car rolling up the drive.

"Saturdays are the best days to start," she says calmly, misunderstanding me on purpose. "There's going to be an open house on Sunday from two to five. I'll need your help."

"Would you like me to dust the couch?" I ask.

My mother glares at me. Donny honks the horn, and I bend to pick up my things. I look at my mother, her hand small on the knife, her hair dripping and quivering as she starts in on the lettuce, pulling the good leaves away from the bad. I decide not to say good-bye.

In the car, I tell Donny about the house and then the scholarship. "Are you excited?" he asks me, even though he knows the answer.

"I'll have three roommates," I say. I reach for his hand. "Are you going to visit me?"

Donny rolls his eyes. "It's only two hours away."

This is true, but it feels farther. Donny drives with one hand and holds my hand until our palms are sticky and we can't feel the pressure on our skin anymore. I want him to say he'll go with me, find a job, save money for school. I want to cut his hair, buy him a suit or even a nice button-down shirt. I want to tell him everyone will understand.

Donny pulls into the Star parking lot and cuts the engine, and we sit still as the car heats.

"Nothing's going to change," Donny says, and I believe him.

That night, Donny does a great show. You'd think it would be the same every night, but it's not. Sometimes the smoke rolls out evenly over the lanes like a piece of cloth, and the laser seems to become different things—a spaceship, a man swimming, someone dancing. Tonight the music's from *Close Encounters of the Third Kind,* and people lean back in the booths, their faces open in the blue light. Donny makes the laser disappear and then reappear in a sweep that washes over us all. He makes it a knife, cutting light into the sky, then a layer of water that lifts above the lanes and spreads itself so thin it's nearly invisible.

I close my eyes and lean my head back and wonder what we look like from space. I see my father leaning to read the lane, gliding forward to roll. *I just want to shoot down the middle,*

I tell him. The music gets louder until the laser breaks apart over the lanes, coming back together into a single glowing point and then goes dark. Everyone yells and claps.

Afterward, I help Leo serve up last beers and popcorns. In the control booth, Donny is shutting things down, the board lighting his face like a ghost. He sees me and waves, and I wave back, and then he turns off the desk light, and I can't see him anymore.

Then it's cash out time. I hurry to the back room so I can get to Leo before Donny does. He's smoking a cigarette, which he quickly puts out because it's against fire regulations to smoke around all the paper plates and napkins. "Tess!" he says, waving at the smoke as if he's just noticed it.

"Leo, I've got to ask you something."

"Ask."

"I got into school."

"I know."

This surprises me and then I realize Donny must have told him. "I want to know if I can come back. In case things don't work out."

"Oh, sure you can, Tess," Leo says. "But you won't." He pats my head with his paw hand, and I feel as if something has broken loose in my ribs, and then I'm crying into the brown polyester warmth of his shoulder until he helps me sit down.

"Breathe, sweetheart," he says. "Just breathe."

Then I feel Donny's hands on my arms, warm. "Let's roll some," he says.

I let him lead me into the dark lanes. We take my favorite one on the end, where I can concentrate. Donny puts change in the jukebox and goes back up to his light board. He puts on the disco ball, white lights circling slow, like stars in a planetarium. I sit down, switch my shoes, pull my AMF out, and turn it in my hands. It's a little sparkling planet, all lakes and waves. I move to the head of the lane, shoes slick like a pillow of air. I pull in a deep breath, inhaling the place, which smells like wood and oil and beer and my father. I balance the ball and let its weight take my arm back, my body moving forward, my hand behind the ball, pushing it through the air. My thumb comes free, and my hand turns into an almost handshake, fingers flicking the skin of the ball as it leaves them, all this in a split second, like air leaving the lungs, like a kiss.

I shut my eyes and bring my father's face close to mine, skin around his gray eyes crinkling. *I'm leaving,* I tell him, as the ball topples the pins. I know from the sound it's a strike.

By the time we get to my house, it's very late. I make Donny stop several houses down the street from mine and turn off his lights. We sit there in the hollow car silence.

"What are we doing?" Donny asks.

"Shh." I get out quietly, shiver in the cool air. "Just wait for me here, OK?"

Donny nods and sits back. On my way down the street, I glance at Mr. Ontero's dark house, the windows small and black. Every room is lit at my house, porch lights glowing over the FOR SALE sign leaning against the steps. My mother passes through the empty living room. She's wearing my pink sundress.

I wait until she walks upstairs and let myself in the front door. There is the lavender duffel bag on the floor, full and zipped, the keys on the counter.

I head down the hallway and grab my backpack, checking for the envelope, my father's shirts, making sure it's all still there, ready. In the kitchen, I hear my mother humming upstairs. I lift her keys slowly from the counter and pull the front door closed behind me.

I take the brick path around the side of the house to the edge of the woods and set down my backpack. The keys are cool in my hand. I hold them up chin level, setting. My arm is trembling, tired but warm. I let it drop, fall back, my feet sliding with long, low strides, my arm swinging forward now, fingers relaxing on the upswing, then releasing the keys, which fly upward for quite a ways because they are lighter than what I'm used to. They land somewhere in the dark trees with a muffled clink of metal. I listen to the quiet air for a moment and then walk back to the car, where Donny is waiting to take me to school.

Graceland

I killed my husband's boss four years after he fired him, which was right after he talked us into moving across the country for a promotion and a raise that never materialized. You'd think I'd be over it by now, and I did, too. But then we saw him in a restaurant in Memphis on Fourth of July weekend three years ago. I'd had to go for a sales meeting, and we had decided to stay the weekend and take our daughter, Alice, to Graceland. Alice loves Elvis, the sequins, the sweet, honeyed songs. I wonder if all girls go through this, like the horse stage. I don't remember it, personally.

So my husband's ex-boss—I'll call him Bob—bounds to our table like a long-lost poker buddy and puts out his small hand (Bob's a small man) and tells my husband what a great surprise it is to see him again. George looks up and doesn't even recognize him at first because that's the way George is; he just moves on and doesn't let the past cling to him the way I do. Bob keeps talking, "Whaddya know, I come out here to retire, just sold the business, and what a great surprise!"

George puts his napkin on the table and stands up, and I think for a moment that he's going to hit him, but then I realize that's what I would do in this situation, not George, who's sweet and never violent. Then I see this friendly smile spreading across George's face and his hand coming up to meet Bob's, and my fingers claw into the arms of the chair as I push myself out of it.

"Bob," I say as I step around the table, so that I'm between him and Alice, who probably knows I'm about to do something before I actually realize it—like when I was a kid and knew when my dad was about to hit a bender again even though it always seemed to surprise my mother. Kids can sense trouble like animals smell storms.

"Bob," I say again because he isn't looking at me yet; he's taking his time the way men do when they've decided a woman isn't relevant or a threat. But then he has to look at me, up at me actually, because I'm wearing heels and pressing my left tit into his right shoulder, leaning into it.

George freezes, the smile on his face like a man holding a pose for a long camera exposure. He begins lifting a finger to signal me because he's seen me get this way before—like the time a cop ticketed me for speeding and I threatened to beat his lying ass, which I'll admit wasn't smart because even though we didn't have Alice then, we did have an ounce of pot under the seat.

"Bob," I say for the third time, just because I'm enjoying saying his name like he's a dog caught peeing on the carpet. "I want you to walk away from this table, and if you ever talk to a member of my family again, I'm going to slit you from asshole to eyeballs."

Bob looks at me, a smile just beginning to work its way through the part of the old brain that decides whether you should fight or fuck or just sit there and lick yourself. I figure he's decided on licking, so I grab his scrotum and the tip of his penis tightly through his seersucker pants, confirming that the equipment is, in fact, in proportion with the rest of the man, and I squeeze.

"I mean it, Bobby," I say softly, trying to convey something like sympathy with my eyes, for the fact that he's so small and so crooked and being victimized by a woman he once propositioned at a cocktail party, a woman who at the time was trying to take the high road in what she could see was a bad situation, a woman who briefly tried to behave with something like grace.

Bob grabs at my arm, but I'm faster. I let go and step back and smile my best cocktail-party smile. He looks at George, who is horrified, and then at Alice, who is short enough to have had a straight-on view of the ball grab. She's just taking it all in, big-eyed. Then Bob turns and walks away, stiffly.

Sometimes I still think about how if I hadn't seen him, he'd still be tooling around those mint-green golf courses they've carved all over the hills of Memphis.

George took Alice to Graceland alone the next day—he was too angry to let me come. "Go get in some bar fights and get it out of your system," he said, and I was mad enough to do it. But people have a way of sensing that, and no one gave me a chance.

Why am I so angry? I've spent up to a hundred and twenty-five dollars an hour trying to answer that question. I could blame it on my weak, bingeing father, but that seems too simple. I could blame it on growing up large for my age, so that I could beat up high school boys when I was in sixth grade, an ability I grew to enjoy, although after the first few times people pretty much left me alone. I could blame it on being a woman because when a woman learns to like fighting, she doesn't do it for sport or to make a point. It isn't a form of communication, the way it can be for men. It's attempted murder every time. I've never quit a fight until someone pulled me off. Putting someone on the ground wasn't enough.

That night I watched the fireworks over Graceland from our hotel room. And that's when I decided how to do it.

I waited nearly a year. All that time I was a seed, a cocoon, waiting to unfurl. I listened to George's lectures about how Alice was afraid of me. I made Alice's lunches before school and talked about how Mommy had a temper she was trying to work on. I don't think she believed me. Meanwhile, I cruised the Internet late at night. I bought fertilizer at the local gardening store, in small quantities, over time. I bought a casing at the army-surplus store. I built the thing in the garage when George was working late and Alice had ballet. I tested one in the country and blew a six-foot crater in some farmer's tobacco field. I waited for business to take me back to Memphis like a spore on the wind.

I had to drive all night, the night I did it. I prayed for an open garage and was blessed with a carport. Then I had to figure out which car to do. I knew Bob had divorced and remarried in the intervening years between when he tried to grab my ass behind the wet bar and this, his last night. I chose the convertible with the bottle of Stetson in the glove compartment and the driver's seat jacked up almost to the steering wheel.

I was in a meeting all of the next day, and the next evening I saw it on the news in the airport as I was waiting on my flight. *Respected retired businessman killed in mob-style blast, car blown up beyond recognition.* It was all I could do to decide whether to cheer or throw up.

For the next few months, I waited. Waited for someone to ask the widow about his enemies, for someone to check the mileage on a certain Alamo rental car, for someone to calculate how an energetic soul could drive from the airport, past Graceland, to a new golf-course development outside of Memphis. A year passed. Then two, and Alice had shifted her interests from Elvis to psychology. Her coloring lightened so that she started looking a lot more like her father, and she started leaving books like *The Anger Within* and *The Heart of Violence* open to certain highlighted passages at my place at the breakfast table. Maybe she knows.

We are all cursed with some kind of weakness. Elvis's was the drugs, a wall of attention always threatening to crush him. Alice's is believing people can change their core nature. George's is kindness, the need to give and receive it.

Mine might just be a lack of patience, or flexibility, or shame. Because I can still say the only thing I regret is not seeing that son of a bitch blow.

Package

Because my grandfather was once a horseback courier (Fort Worth Rough Riders) and views the modern postal system with suspicion and disdain, he had elected the assurance that I, and I alone, could sign for the package. Therefore, the woman who took my call informed me, I would have to be present for the delivery.

"But I can't do that. I work," I said, as I stuck the yellow delivery slip on one finger, then the next. I imagined my grandfather's jaw set in a serious line as he filled out the necessary paperwork, his stiff fingers moving across the page. I saw the rows of gray desks in my department, the sliver of lake view beyond the Flats, the stacks of magazines on every subject, from *Professional Car Washing* to *Executive Renderer,* waiting for key words to be discovered like scattered keepsakes and returned to their owners.

"You can arrange to pick it up at the nearest service center," the woman said. The connection crackled; other voices jabbered faintly in the background. I made the arrangements and got directions to the service center. The next day, I left work early, happy to have an excuse. I had been unproductive all day, ignoring clip bundles accumulating on my desk, managing to appear busy while perusing the Internet for plane tickets I did not plan to purchase. My daily horoscope had prescribed travel to ease restlessness, and though this advice could apply to a great many people not born between the summer solstice and late July, I believed it relevant to my life.

I followed the directions to the service center west of Brecksville, an area unfamiliar to me, as it has until only recently been farms. I drove slowly on the newly tarred roads between industrial parks, trying to get my bearings. Once my parents had taken me to a dairy in this area, where we ate soft vanilla ice cream and watched cows pace through the waving grass.

By the time I had arrived at the service center, a low, gray cube on a vast spread of blacktop, I felt a twinge of annoyance. Why couldn't my grandfather have allowed me to simply sign the little slip and reattach it to my front door? He has always been a difficult man, according to my mother, a quality I have observed on every visit to his small, stuffy house in Lubbock, Texas. Alone or with company, he lives undeterred from his patterns and oblivious to those of other people—to bed at 8:00 P.M., up at 4:00 A.M. for as long as my memory, banging pans in the kitchen to boil coffee on the stove. Now that my grandmother is gone, there is no one to influence his habits. Lubbock suits him, it being one the most difficult places to live, with its sweltering heat and ice storms and sand storms that rise out of the west like a blurred yellow cord, whipping the surfaces off buildings and the leaves off trees, the fine granules sticking to the skin, dusting the shelves of locked cabinets.

As I parked my car, I remembered I had once had bad luck with this parcel service when I sent my mother more than a dozen books she never received. She was in Texas that summer, tending to her mother as she was dying. I called several carriers—this one was the least expensive by only a few dollars. But at the time, money was scarce; my husband had just left me to marry a coworker of his, a lean blonde woman whom I had met once and who liked to ski; this is one of the few things I know about her. My mother wanted to come stay with me but of course could not leave her own mother. Painful as it was to have my marriage fail, it was somehow harder still to tell friends and relatives the run-of-the-mill truth of the office romance, the broken marriage vows, the man starting over in the middle of life.

The books never arrived. I considered it part of my general luck, careful plans disappearing as if they had never existed.

So I was already leery when I parked my car and walked up the two-tiered ramp into the wall of air-conditioning and took my place in line. It went fast enough; there were only two people ahead of me: a boy, maybe sixteen, with a tangled, bleached bob, and a middle-aged white woman in a green dress mailing a package and chatting with the middle-aged black woman at the register. "I just tell them if they lay up in the bed and don't get up to say hello and how are you to everyone, they walk to school, and they don't get any lunch money," the woman at the register said.

"Now I like that policy," the other woman said. "I'm gonna try that on *my* kids."

"Let me know how it goes," the register lady said. They were obviously both enjoying their public banter. The customer laughed and gathered her purse, late afternoon sun on her face as she walked out.

The kid with the bob had something to pick up. A woman came from the back room, took his ticket and mine, and retreated behind the gray door again.

My grandfather had called me at seven on a Saturday

morning, six o'clock his time, to tell me he was going to market to post a parcel to me. That was exactly how he said it, stubborn in keeping his language from another time. I thought of asking him not to call so early, but he rarely calls, as he is mindful of the high long-distance rates, so I decided not to complain. Plus, he is ninety-three, and I believe he will not live much longer, and so I hated to think of chastising him during what might have been our last conversation. I had thought of that possibility for nearly twenty years—the last phone call, the last visit—long before my grandmother died her slow death in the back bedroom, staring at her choked rosebushes by the window. But he sounded energized that morning and had certainly been up for hours. Caring for my grandmother had nearly killed him, but he was rejuvenated as a widower and has rebuffed several offers of marriage from widows living in the new condos in town, which he laughingly reports during our periodic conversations. I often wonder if he's making fun of me for not having any new offers of my own.

"It's a surprise," he said, when I asked him what the package was. This caught me off guard. He had never once sent a surprise, nor had I ever heard of his discussing surprises. For years he had sent checks to my parents for my brother's and my Christmas and birthday gifts, twenty-five dollars each, year after year, even during the years when my mother wasn't speaking to him or to her mother, for reasons that were never disclosed. He said he didn't know what to buy children, having never had any toys himself. This always angered my mother, who had chosen to know things not revealed to her in childhood—and not just material things, though she and my father live well, in a tastefully decorated Tudor house in Shaker Heights filled with Oriental rugs and pottery. The carefulness and grace with which she decorates and dresses and entertains all come from a desire to know and give more than what she started with.

I told my grandfather that I would look forward to the package, insisting on using my word, and after that he was anxious to get off the phone, probably to avoid spending too much on the call. Lately he had been giving things away—stocks, a brass bed my grandmother had bought on one of their two visits to Cleveland at an antique store downtown. This was when I was a kid and the antique shops on Euclid Avenue were called junk shops. My grandmother, taller than my grandfather then and taller than the shopkeeper, too, her hazel Cherokee eyes narrowed in combat, wheedled and demanded and walked away and returned, feigning anger at being taken advantage of until the shopkeeper had given her half his asking price for it—twenty-five dollars. I sleep in this bed now. I had the bed appraised, and it is now worth more than fifteen hundred dollars. I remember stepping out onto the street that day, holding my grandmother's hand, the purchase complete, the delivery to Lubbock arranged. It was early spring, the light jumpy and gray over Lake Erie, and my grandmother laughed and recounted her triumph again and again on the drive home.

My grandfather, I knew, was planning for his death, parceling out his belongings as pragmatically as he had written our gift checks every year. I sat in the bed and cried after that phone call, feeling closer to death than I ought to at thirty-nine, or rather, feeling that there was not much to live for, and for my weakness in the face of such thoughts. For my grandfather, there is no turning back. He is healthy and frail at the same time; his hip bones jut under his belt, his trousers gap, and his wrists are pale and wide compared with his narrow arms. For me, there are still supposedly many options, many turns in the road.

The woman came out from the back room shaking her head. "Your package is still on the truck," she said to the young man with the bob. "You might be able to get it if you wait until they come in."

"But I got a notice," he said.

"Did you call?" she asked patiently, as if talking to a child. Her eyes were kind. He shook his head. He was a child.

"How long will it be?" he asked, tugging his hair behind his ears. A wedding band gleamed on his finger. It surprised me; he looked too young.

"About thirty minutes."

He sighed, but there was nothing to be done. I felt a secret sense of superiority because I had called. I had planned. I understood how the world worked.

"I'll be right back," the woman said to me. I nodded, smiling my best professional smile, the one I use at work, at the grocery store, when greeting other walkers while out with Elsa, my aging black Lab. I thought of Elsa, lying in her kennel, sleeping probably, but perhaps looking out the window, knowing it was the time of day when I should appear, or perhaps not thinking specifically of me but waiting all the same.

The woman returned quickly, and I gathered my keys and sunglasses, preparing to receive the package and leave. But then I saw her lips were pressed together, and she had started to shake her head again. "Yours is still on the truck, too," she said.

"But I called," I said, too loudly, perhaps.

"You did?" She seemed surprised.

"Yes, I did, yesterday, to arrange it."

"Well, let me call the driver and see what I can find out."

She left again, and I leaned against the counter, suddenly exhausted. I had been sitting all day, but I wanted to sit down, to close my eyes. A Hispanic man dressed in a repair-shop jumpsuit with the name GERALDO stitched on the breast pocket came in with several thick, spiral-bound notebooks. He purchased a box and began packing the notebooks with shredded paper and clear tape, provided free. His cell phone rang, and he began talking loudly in Spanish and laughing. Another man came in, about mid-sixties, closely cropped gray hair, wearing a pale-blue shirt and pinstriped slacks. I watched him produce his slip.

"I was here earlier, and they told me it would be here after 6:30," he said to the register lady in a genial voice that filled the square room. I looked at the clock. It was 6:40; I had been there twenty minutes.

The register lady went to the back this time, the other lady already occupied with my missing package. It didn't take her long to return empty-handed. "I'm sorry," she said, and the man pressed his palm to his forehead.

"I can't believe it," he said. His voice seemed too high-pitched for his body, slightly effeminate. "They called me at work and at home to tell me."

"Well, I'll call the supervisor and see if he knows anything," she said and smiled, a slight dip of sarcasm in her voice at the idea of a supervisor knowing something, and the man rolled his eyes, smiling, too.

"Yeah, right," he said.

I am a supervisor. I supervise four young women, one older woman, and one man my age, readers for a clipping service downtown. The company reviews twenty thousand publications a month for public-relations firms looking to justify their existence to clients. Everyone in our group gets along well. I package the clips into bundles, tag them with computer-generated labels, and send them to the firms. The packages always arrive. In fact, I can't remember even one being lost.

I began to wonder if I was supposed to continue waiting or if the woman had said she would call me. I stared out the rectangular window. Across a closely mown, bright-green field and the wide street, there was a long brick building surrounded by a razor wire-topped fence. I wondered what would happen if the world were to end and we, the people in this room, were the only ones to survive. How would our lives be together? How would we couple to keep our species alive? I studied each person: the stocky Geraldo, who was placing his package on the rollers and deciding whether to send it one- or two-day delivery (I wanted to grab the package from him and warn him to send it by another carrier); the slim-hipped boy with a bob, now coming in from smoking a cigarette; the two female employees, plus another one whose arm was the only thing I could see through the doorway into the back room, moving a mouse in small circles on a brightly colored pad. The older man in the pinstriped slacks was frustrated. I wanted to comfort him but could think of nothing to say.

"I came all the way across town for this," he said to the younger man.

"Where do you work?" the kid asked.

"At Heighton's, men's shoes."

"Oh, really?" the boy said. "I need to stop by there sometime. To get clothes, I mean." The older man looked disappointed. "I used to shop at Brooks Brothers, but I think Heighton's is better," he said then, but the older man was already looking out the window at the cars passing on the new highway.

The woman looking for my package came back again. "I'm still on hold," she said.

I looked at the floor. "You know, this is really important," I said, already feeling peevish for saying it. Who didn't think their packages were important, those parts of ourselves we send out across the country, the world even? She had heard it all before. I thought as fast as I could. "Look, can I just sign now, and you deliver it to my home?"

"Well," she said, taking the ratty sticky note that I had pulled from my front door and remembered to stuff in my bag and carry to work so I would have it to show here at this place, which had once been a field. "Mr. Milton paid more to have you sign for it at the time of delivery," the woman said.

I bit my lip. I could hear my mother's voice, *Yeah, but he used the cheapest carrier he could find. Spend a dime to save a penny.*

"My grandfather doesn't realize I work," I said, trying to smile. It felt more like a grimace.

"Can another family member sign for it?"

I shook my head, making a note never to ask anyone that question.

"Can we deliver it to your office?" She was trying to be helpful, but it wasn't helpful at all.

"I work on the tenth floor of a building downtown, and I park two blocks away," I said. "It will be too heavy to carry that far." I had remembered that detail just then, the only clue he would give me, that it was large and heavy. I assumed it was another piece of furniture.

"Well, I'll ask the supervisor if you can sign now, but I don't think he'll let me."

"Oh, forget it," I said. I walked out, red in the face, wanting to cry. I had left the slip with the woman. But I felt too defeated and embarrassed to go back for it.

I got home at seven, walked Elsa, made dinner—pasta and green beans, enough for several meals, which I packed in plastic tubs and stuffed in the freezer—and watched television until I felt sleepy enough to go to bed.

The next day, I was a productive worker, organized, cheerful even. I thought about calling the parcel place, but I was too busy. I did such a good job that I decided to let myself leave at 6:00 instead of trying to avoid being the first one out. I dislike the hypocrisy of pretending to work late, but there is an unspoken understanding that supervisors at our firm are supposed to stay as long as their department workers do, and keeping my job is important, with the benefits, the relative security.

When I got home, the delivery truck was in the drive, and the delivery man was at the door. I parked on the street so as not to block him. I was surprised to see him; on the way home, I had been imagining the complaint letter I would write for the lack of organization, my time wasted, even the previous non-delivery of my books. But I also knew I wouldn't write any letter, even if the package came to me in pieces.

The delivery man saw me, waved, rolled open the back of the truck. "Good timing!" he said. He was cheerful, tanned, good looking. He jumped inside and dragged the package to the edge of the truck, hopped out, and struggled to lift it. It was a trunk wrapped in duct tape.

"Here, let me help you," I said.

"That's OK," he grunted. "Just open your door. I'll put this inside for you."

The trunk hit the floor of my living room with a muffled thud. "There you go," said the delivery man, Chuck, according to his shirt. He smiled brightly, as if trying to think of something more to say.

"Thank you," I said, and then I realized he was waiting for a tip. I fumbled around in my purse, found a dollar, handed it to him. He left, unimpressed. I had thought for a moment he was flirting with me. *What was I thinking?* I asked myself. I am no longer the slender girl I now see only in pictures. I put on weight after I got married, and never could drop it, though my features are regular and my skin has held up well. I watched the truck back down my driveway and realized I had stopped expecting men to look at me.

The trunk sat diagonally in front of my couch, the first purchase I had made after Bill left. The trunk looked like a weathered coffee table; in fact, that's what I decided to do with it later that evening, when I had gone through its contents—what I expected to be junk my grandfather wanted to discard—and placed each item around the house, out in the open. I touched its battered skin, leaned down to inspect the latch. I could smell my grandparents' house along the crack of the lid, a combination of mothballs and rooms never aired out.

Before I opened it, I let Elsa out of her kennel. She stepped out slowly, stretched, leaned against me. She showed up not long after Bill left, as if pulled by the gravity of my loneliness. I never thought I would be grateful to an animal, but I am, the way I was to the first Elsa I knew.

Elsa was actually my best girlfriend until we were both nine, when her parents moved from Cleveland to Dayton. She was beautiful, with blond hair and fine skin that seemed to have a light behind it, especially at her cheeks and the skin on the backs of her knees. She lived down the street from me, and we ate every lunch together and played every afternoon. I saw her as my savior because she was so gentle and well liked, while I got constant "doesn't follow directions" comments on report cards for forgetting homework assignments and was teased by boys who made fun of my buck teeth, later corrected with braces. Elsa was sweet but fiercely loyal, and to make fun of me around her was to lose her approval, a power she had that I had somehow been born without. She was my protector and seemed almost motherly, even then. I am sure she is a mother now.

Elsa the stray that showed up after Bill left, during that time blurred by Zoloft and the alcohol I was supposed to avoid, had these same qualities. She was graceful, quiet, concerned. I ran an ad in the paper, even though I wanted to keep her, but only one drunk man called to claim her and refused to get off the phone until I had to hang up on him. I took her to the vet after a week, and as the young doctor examined her, I talked about how it was a big adjustment for me to get a dog; I'd never had one before but had always wanted one. I didn't tell him about my husband who had run away. Instead, I talked about my busy life, trying to make it sound full and exciting. "I'm worried, though," I said. "I work all the time, and I don't know if she'll get enough exercise."

"Oh, she's middle-aged," the vet said. "She'll be perfect for you."

I knew immediately what he meant, that because she wasn't young, she wouldn't need as much exercise, but I couldn't stop myself from glancing at him, just to be sure. Worse, I could see his wanting to explain, to make sure I wouldn't take offense, because to him, I was middle-aged. I never took Elsa to him again, even though he was good with her.

Elsa walked with me to the mailbox, stopping to sniff tree roots as I looked through the day's delivery. There was a letter from Teresa, my friend from graduate school and the only person I correspond with anymore.

I opened and read the letter in the driveway. Her son

Thomas had learned to pick the childproof kitchen-cabinet latches with a fork, launching a new safety challenge. *He is changing every day. Sometimes I think I can see him growing.* Then a suggestion of a cruise, maybe to Alaska. *I know you get enough snow, but I want to see those glaciers in the middle of the summer.* My first reaction was to reject the idea because cruises make me think of huge, floating shuffleboards for retirees or Vegas-style singles' bars. But then, I thought, as I held the front door open for Elsa, maybe that wouldn't be so bad. Maybe my horoscope was correct.

Elsa waited patiently for me at the door while I pulled her leash from the nail in the storeroom. I thought of the glaciers, and of meeting a man, and of how nice it would be to remarry and for Bill to hear about it. Petty but nice. I clipped the leash on Elsa's collar and led her back outside. I had finally steered Bill into marriage, I realize now. He had never had to worry about whether I wanted him, whether I would stay with him. On the few occasions during our eight-year marriage when I got angry with him, he told me stories about his father. One night his father had held him by his heels from a bridge to punish him for complaining about wanting to go home. My mother and Teresa think I married him to save him, but I believe it was the other way around.

When Bill left, Teresa said I should have the children I'd always wanted, the ones Bill had refused because of his abusive childhood. "You're better off having children without him," she said. "Look at me," she now adds since Thomas's father has moved away. When she says it, I think of the green jade frog on the tall wooden pedestal in her foyer, which her son toppled soon after he learned to crawl; the scar on his forehead is now very small. "You can do it, too," she says, almost every time we talk. As if motherhood is a cure.

Elsa and I worked our way down Willow to Carlsbad to Lilac Street and back up Willow. Sprinklers turned on freshly mowed lawns in front of rows of red-brick houses, cars clicked and cooled at the tops of driveways. It was trash day, so there were emptied pairs of rubbish and recycling bins at the curbs. Children yelled from backyards. The light was low and golden in the leaves.

Life has gotten simpler after the divorce in ways I don't really mind, now that I am over the shock and pain. After a while, I welcomed the control over how the furniture would be arranged, what groceries I would buy—issues Bill and I had fiercely argued. I had thought marriage would make my life easier and more complete at the same time, but it had done neither. It was not so much a function of who Bill was as who I was. I enjoyed the acceptance being married brought me— the couples-only invitations to dinner parties, the assumed legitimacy so that I could have a conversation with any man I wanted and no one would raise an eyebrow, take me for a desperate single woman. But I had in fact become a desperate married woman, always angling for attention from a man who I guess never loved me, not with any real passion. At twenty-nine, I had thought it was time to get married, then it was time to buy a house, then to have children. At thirty-nine, I can see that life is a process of accumulating and letting go, of expansion and contraction.

It is memory that stays with us, that compels us to think and rethink the past, to try to find places for what is left. Bill and I were perhaps too similar. I have always been overly neat, "puttering," as my mother puts it, to avoid more important activities, like traveling or finding someone new to add to my life. But Bill was compulsive. He folded even the smallest item of clothing precisely, whereas I simply threw my underwear in my drawer, secretly thrilling at my few nonputtering habits, hoping to coax them into more areas of my life. Bill wiped off the bottoms of coffee cups before placing them in the cabinet and yelled at me when I didn't. Now when I pull them from the dishwasher and put them away dripping, I still feel a furtive pleasure.

When Elsa and I returned, the living room was filled with the smell of the trunk, mostly that of mothballs. I felt a pang of resentment at its dark presence, at the inconvenience it had caused me and would probably continue to cause me, what with cleaning it out, finding a place for it, writing my grand-father a thank-you note for the trouble—his and mine.

I fed Elsa and heated my meal, leftovers from the night before. Standing by the microwave, a glass of white wine cool in my hand, I observed the trunk. It was three or four feet long, a couple of feet tall, and about that deep. It was black, maybe a dark brown. I stepped closer to inspect it. It was cased in leather, which was dry and cracked and held in place by bands of metal, also blackened with age and use and then finally disuse. I imagine it sat in the garage for years. Clearly it had been my grandmother's. Faded labels on its back and side announced Fort Worth, St. Louis, Chicago, Pittsburgh, Washington, D.C., even Cleveland—all places my grand-mother had worked, transferring around as an operator for the telephone company when it was called Ma Bell, before she married my grandfather.

Of course my grandfather, not one for delicate or attractive packaging, had wrapped duct tape fully around the body of the trunk, six or seven times, and had complemented it with sev-eral rounds of string. I put my glass of wine on the plant stand and eased the trunk onto its back. It wasn't easy to do, and I wondered how he'd managed it. He had always been very strong, a quality I remembered from my childhood, when he would grab my wrist if I displeased him until I felt as if my bones would crack. He had either not thought of or not cared how the tape might damage the old leather. He was of the school who used what he had to make things work: coat hangers to fashion the antenna on a truck he gave my parents years ago, and later, my grandmother's diapers to insulate a leaking pipe. He was not a sentimental man. I both disliked and envied this quality in him.

The microwave beeped, and I stood the trunk back up. I ate my meal, pulled a knife from the drawer, kneeled in front of the trunk again. The tape had gone gooey from the heat of a week's transit in trucks. The hinges were stiff. I eased the lid back until it stayed open and pulled out tightly packed handfuls of plastic bags and crumpled newspapers. I was beginning to think he had just sent me a stuffed trunk when I saw a porcelain arm, a sliver of calico poking from a grocery bag.

There were nine dolls in all. Five were Madame Alexander dolls, collector's items, still in their boxes, with tags on their wrists, which meant they would perhaps still be valuable, even if a little moldy. Two were matching porcelain dolls, about a foot tall, with rag bodies and shiny white faces and limbs. Their red hair was painted into a chignon with curls on top, like Lucille Ball's. They wore matching dresses that I remembered my grandmother making the summer she tried to teach me to sew. I had been an eager but slow student, unable to understand the properties of the cloth, the way it would hang with a certain cut.

I remembered the small sewing machine she had used, bending over it, her fingers slow with arthritis but skilled. She had talked all the while, telling how the nuns at the mission school had taught her to write cursive like a lady so she could marry well and have a good life, how she had won a competition in high school with a dress she had made, the dime haircuts she had given in her neighborhood to make a little extra when times were tough, about the flower shop that she had grown from nothing but a few arrangements in the garage. I know now that she was trying to talk to me about self-sufficiency, about surviving with grace.

I pulled from the packing material a rag doll she had also made, with a round sweet face and orange hair, kept at their house for my visits. At the bottom was a small porcelain baby doll that I had never seen before, cracked in several places, I imagined, from the weight of the other dolls. I set it on the counter, sifting smaller pieces from the newspapers and placing them next to its body for repair.

I took the Madame Alexander dolls out of their boxes, lined them up on the couch, reacquainting myself with them. Little Girl Pink, in her gauzy pink gown, and Little Boy Blue, with his velvet blue knickers and matching jacket, were easy to remember, as were the second two, Napoleon and Josephine. And I recognized Scarlet O'Hara's white ball gown, which she wore before she was married, before she lost everything and rebuilt it into something altogether different and completely hers.

When I was a child, I had believed strongly in the secret lives of dolls and had tried many times to sneak down the hallway to my bedroom to enter their private existence before it dispersed in the quiet air. My grandmother had collected these dolls supposedly for me, but they had never left her bedroom, and I remembered staring at them and wanting to play with them on visits as a child. Back then, they had stood behind the locked hand-blown glass cabinet of her secretary, and I was told that they were not for children and were just for looking at, a concept beyond my comprehension at that time.

One day she had relented, during the summer she had tried to teach me to sew, allowing me to arrange them on her bed. She left me alone with them for only a few minutes. I was about six or seven and just getting handy with scissors. Maybe I was thinking of my grandmother's stories of neighborhood haircuts, maybe I was thinking of nothing at all beyond the pleasure of snipping at the shining strands of Josephine's hair, watching them fall slowly onto the bedspread. But when my grandmother came back, I remember her screaming and then my grandfather, their faces large with anger. And then my mother appeared, and she was screaming, too, only not at me but at them. I never touched the dolls again, even when visiting as an adult, and no one ever spoke of what happened. On one visit, I noticed a cap had appeared on Josephine's head, beaded to match her dress.

The cap, I could now see, was attached to her head with a thin piece of flesh-colored elastic that ran under her chin. I had not thought of the incident for years, and remembering it again—the pink walls of the bedroom, the slowly falling hair—made me pause before lifting the velvet cap. The hair was untouched in front but cut nearly to the scalp in back. I ran my fingers over it as if to read something in its texture. My grandmother had cried after her initial outburst. I know she stared at the dolls for thousands of hours before she died.

I wondered if my grandfather had thought of that day, too, as he prepared the trunk for transit, if he saw me in his mind's eye, knees red and pressed with the pattern of the bedspread, nylon hairs sticking to my face, crying. Probably he thought I was spoiled, destructive, unable to appreciate even the finest things. Maybe he wondered what the world would come to, with children like me destined to run it.

I thought of calling my grandfather to thank him for the dolls, but at nearly eight o'clock his time, he might already be asleep or watching the TV, dentures soaking in a glass. Maybe he had sent the dolls as reconciliation, a gesture that I was finally ready for them. More likely, he had sent them because he is a practical man, and he will die soon, and he would rather control where pieces of his past go than let someone else decide.

I smoothed the dolls' skirts, straightened their jackets, bent their soft legs outward so they could sit. I sat across from them and cradled my empty wineglass. Outside, a streetlamp flicked on, and the light pooled silvery white on the grass. I would stay awake for hours yet, breathing quietly, willing myself to be there and not there at the same time, waiting for a signal, a sign of life.

Dough

The word for the day is scarf. I've got the rest of the summer, and I figure that's a good start. Right now Nellie Larue—that's my grandmother—is trying to fold the scarf, but it keeps slipping from her fingers, making Nellie frown in a way that crinkles the corners of her round, sky-blue eyes and flares the rosebud nostrils of her nose, determined little mouth now trying to form the word again, but what comes out instead is "Phsss."

"Scarf," I prompt.

"Phsst!"

"Let's have lunch," I suggest.

Nellie's not one to give in easily, but this time she lets the scarf float to the floor. She takes my arm then and allows me to guide her down the hallway to the kitchen. Chin lifted, she is a picture of serenity, the slightest hitch in her step all that's left of the stroke. That and not being able to talk or write. She glides along, all five feet and two inches of her erect, ankles, hips, rib cage lifting from the floor like the dancer she was before marrying the studio instructor and bearing six children—always a bun in the oven back then!—she used to say when she could remember how to talk. My gay grandfather Rodolpho loved all of his children and indulged them as much as he could on the small income from the studio, the best one in western Ohio, where farm girls entertained fantasies of the stage. In his heyday, there were reports of young women twirling *chaines tours* down cornrows instead of helping with harvest. But the farmers paid him with sweaty, creased bills because their wives demanded it—The Dance, as he and Nellie called it, made their daughters straight backed and marriageable—and they even forgave him for loving other men. Though that part of the deal went down quietly during buying trips to Cincinnati for new music or barre equipment.

I know all this from my mother, Nadia (yes, named after the Russian dancer), the youngest of the six, because Rodolpho's dead and Nellie's words get trapped in her throat like little birds fluttering at her lips to escape.

I am cutting off the crust of Nellie's Wonder Bread, boiled egg, and mayonnaise sandwich while she waits at the table, feet tapping a four-two count on one chair leg. Every day we get a different bread from my boyfriend, Charles the baker—sourdough, focaccia, and my favorite, potato bread, but Nellie will have none of it. She sneers at him and calls him names with her eyes because he's big and occasionally clumsy—for Nellie, there's no greater crime. But she can't tell anyone that he spends the night, sneaking out early in the morning to warm the ovens, leaving flour dust traces everywhere like a giant moth. And as much as I would like for Nellie to speak again, it would be problematic if she were to tell my loving but strict mother about Charles staying with us instead of in his apartment down the street from the bakery. He is, after all, twenty-four, and I am only seventeen and on summer break before my senior year of high school.

Nevertheless, I work with Nellie every day on words. I bought flash cards, and in the afternoons before her nap, we

practice. After lunch, we sit in the double swing under the oak
tree in Nellie's flower-bordered backyard. I hold up cards and
say the words: kite, boat, cap, dog. "Now you," I say. Nellie
looks amused, blue eyes bright as new dimes. She thinks this is
some big joke. She winks at me and doesn't even try to say
anything. So today I get crafty. *"Sissonne doublée,"* I say, listing
one of her favorite steps—you start in fifth position, right foot
front, and spring onto the left foot *en pointe,* while slowly
drawing up the right leg and extending it to any height—you
wouldn't believe how strong you have to be to do this. *"Simple,
ouverte, fermée,"* I say, adding some variations. Nellie closes her
eyes and tips her head back, the downy skin of her forehead
delicate as a flower. Swooning in the memory, I'll guess, of
pirouettes on the diagonal across the waxed floor of the studio,
spotting *pointe* shoes hanging from a nail in the corner, which
returned with her from a brief pro gig with the New York City
Ballet (the satin worn off the plaster toes, the ankle ribbons
she stitched gray and frayed, the arch bridge broken from her
many perfect landings), a line of big-boned farm girls from
Rising Sun watching her with crossed freckled arms and
grudging, wishful stares. Maybe she's thinking of that or of the
children who came one after the other, now scattered around
the country with their own families, or of her farmer relatives
who no longer recognize me when I go out running errands
for her while her nurse is on vacation.

Nellie's tired now, so I help her back inside, down the hallway to her room, and into bed. The offending scarf is still on
the floor, which I pick up and put away. Handmade lace curtains web the light. I tuck her in and call my mother to tell her
all is well, my pulse already rising, a warm yeast, because
Charles will be home before long, and he'll slip quietly up the
stairs to my bedroom, our bedroom, sleeping a floury sleep

until I wake him to make love and guide him downstairs for dinner.

It's dangerous, this relationship, not the least because my mother is a paralegal and doesn't see the humor in how Charles and I met. She's not impressed by the fact that he's entirely self-supporting, working for this little bakery, which is a lot more than any guy my age can say. When I tried to talk to my mother about Charles and how sweet he is—and I mean that; he tastes sugary—she said things like "pervert" and "statutory rape."

We met, by the way, when I ran into him on my bike as he was carrying out a three-foot-tall wedding cake for delivery to my Aunt Twyla's wedding, her third. We were both late. He never saw me coming. My bike tipped to one side, and I fell into the cake; it was like a creamy blanket, and the fall didn't even hurt. Charles fell on his back and lay there for several moments, staring dazed at the red-and-white-striped awning. His thick legs stuck straight out, one foot next to my hip. I watched his deep chest rise and fall. He was a slab of a man, solid in ways a teenaged boy can't hope to be unless he's fat. His skin was pale with a blond dusting of hair on his arms that looked like spun sugar. He sat up and looked at me and the cake, and he looked so sad I thought he might cry. "Are you OK?" he asked me, his brown eyes wide with concern.

I looked down at my icing-covered arms and legs, licked some off my hand. I was wearing a dress of fluffed sugar. "I'm fine," I said. "I'm sorry." I felt terrible about the accident but also warm under his gaze. There was a little blood on my knee, and it swirled pink in the icing. I was in love, and when I looked back up at Charles, at the smile spreading on his face, the icing like pearls in his light brown hair, I could tell he was, too.

For now, my mother believes I have followed her wishes and ended things with the baker, as she calls him, when she's not calling him a criminal. Not that I tried to hide it from her until this summer—I even invited him to the junior prom, which was how she found out in the first place and began threatening me with terms like "reform school" and "house arrest." But I don't believe her. My peaceful father would never allow it.

And then there's this photograph, which Nellie once pulled from the bottom of her mold-dotted dresser drawer and showed me: a publicity shot of my mother in a Vegas showgirls lineup. She's in the curve of stars fanning out from the moon. She wears a huge feathery star on her head and one tiny star over each nipple. She wears a tiny bikini bottom with a fringe of sparkly comet trails. She is smiling and hopeful and young, and you can't see the woman who would later tell her daughter to deny love.

I tuck this away like Nellie tucks away words. I'm convinced Nellie doesn't have to be like this forever. I believe she knows more than she lets on. For example, today on the lawn, I showed her a flash card of the word "bird," and she looked right over at a blue jay that was bullying a squirrel. Which means she can read, and the doctors said that would probably never happen.

"I'm on to you," I say, which is what my mother has often said to me.

Nellie winks at me. Then she sighs deeply, looks up at the cloud-ruffled sky, and says, "Tu-tus."

One evening a week later, Nellie's asleep as darkness gathers under the trees and a cool damp rises from the grass. Moths bump against the screen behind me and fly in shaky circles, dazed. A lawn mower hums down the street. I hear Charles turning in bed upstairs and decide it's time to wake him. He sleeps on his back in the wood-framed bed, the mattress swayed with his weight. Three children slept sideways across this bed once, and my mother was one of them, the smallest, always stuck in the middle. I crawl in next to him, press my face against his neck, which of course smells of bread. I run my tongue along the line of his jaw and taste butter. He opens his eyes, and we smile at each other.

"Nellie said 'bicycle' today," I say. The room has turned that lovely summer evening green-gray, the light soft on the wall.

"That makes almost a paragraph since you moved in," Charles says. "Maybe it's a secret message?" He means to be encouraging. He kisses my forehead.

"What did you bake today?" I ask.

"All French breads—*baguettes, croissants,*" he says, using appropriate pronunciation, the sign of a professional. He lists some more, gazing at the ceiling, and I think of each as a ballet step—*baguettes* are quick leaps; *croissants* are turns. The bread for today is on the kitchen table, wrapped in cheesecloth, still warm. Charles turns on one elbow to face me, and I prop on the opposite elbow, mirroring him, our bellies touching.

"What if we got married?" he asks me. His eyes are dark as chocolate. My heartbeat quickens. I realize I want to sink my teeth into his skin, devour him. I think of telling my girl-friends. I think of Aunt Twyla, her first, teenaged husband, her three marriages. "Well?" he says. He's smiling now.

I kiss him, run my tongue inside his lip, hunting sugar. "Are you asking me?" I ask back.

"Yes," he says.

This is what I want forever. He pulls my hand to his rising

cock. I stroke it through his flour-dusted khakis, and right
then I'm thinking I'd like to die in this room, I'm thinking
there's no place I'd rather be than in this big, slant-floored
house of high ceilings and tall windows, in the arms of this
baker who brings me fresh bread every day—what will happen
when Nellie's nurse comes back from vacation and I have to
move back into my parents' house and go back to school? I
push this thought out of my mind and roll on top of Charles,
pulling his pants and boxers past his hips, kicking my shorts
and underwear off my ankles. I fit him inside of me and lean
over him, closing my eyes as his hands knead my arms and
shoulders and breasts, heating me.

There's no going back, I think, once you've tasted a certain
level of freedom. You can't compromise anymore. You can
make your peace, which is what I think my mother did—how
else do you explain the leap from showgirl to paralegal? How
else can you explain the choice of my careful father, who I
know for a fact has never been out west because he's always
made the point of saying, "One of these days I'm going to
cross the Mississippi just to say I have."

We could add to this a list of other things my father has
never done that my mother is willing to risk. For example,
sneaking into Nellie's house later that same evening while
we're all asleep, Nellie in her sleigh bed and Charles and I in
the children's bed (the bunk beds for the boys since discarded
and the third bedroom converted to a sewing room and studio
for Nellie, who danced there and taught privately after
Rodolpho died—even now, I'm convinced, she could word-
lessly turn a room full of sullen, clumsy children into bending,
light-hipped, long-necked dancers). How does my mother
manage the cranky porch boards, the gossipy front screen and

steps? She's a dancer, of course, we all are; every one of Nellie and Rodolpho's six children studied The Dance, boys included (which is probably why they left town, to save their sons from a similar fate). My mother could perform *temps leve en tournant* and land silently on floorboards every time. And I learned, too. Right before Rodolpho died, he told me I had a spine balanced like a strip of silk above my hips and that I could do whatever I wanted with my body.

But my mother has an entirely different message, standing in the doorway, finding Charles and me intertwined like one of the soft pretzels he bakes for the ballpark. "Get out!" she stage-yells for maximum effect.

Charles sits up as if burned, accidentally elbowing me in the neck. I cough and choke, words trapped in my throat like Nellie, so I can't say anything as Charles grabs his pants and tries to shimmy into them under the sheets, entirely unsuccessfully, with my mother standing in the doorway, a mean smile saying, *I've seen better.* Charles snags his shirt, while I gurgle at him, trying to tell him to stay. He's on his feet now, and my mother's so triumphant, detective that she is, that she forgets to get out of his way. They stare at each other. I stand up, too, pulling the bedsheet around me. "Charles!" I finally manage.

He looks at me and then at my mother. Something changes in his face; he composes himself. "I want to marry her," he says, and I thrill at being talked about—I am *her,* and I exist for him all the time.

Nadia looks at me. I expect her to ask me, *Are you sure you love him?* Like on TV. But instead she laughs. "You want to marry a child?" she asks Charles. "Go ahead. I give you guys two years. Tops." She turns to me and says, "We saved a little for your college. You can have it in the morning." She looks at me; I can tell she's waiting. She's hoping she scared me, that I'll back out right then. Have I mentioned she's beautiful? She's small and blonde, like Nellie, with porcelain skin, quick movements, and snapping blue eyes.

I focus on the edge of the floor for balance like a sailor hunting the horizon. I always think about my mother's beauty when we're angry because it surprises me how a woman who looks like a girl can be so tough. I'm worried that if I look at her I'll do something crazy, like try to bite her perfect little nose.

"Loreen," she says to me. No, my mother didn't continue Nellie's tradition of naming her children after dancers. She always explained that she wanted me to feel free to do what I wanted with my life. But there are exceptions, indemnities. Now she wants reconciliation, she wants me to see the wisdom in what she's doing, the craziness in what I'm doing—she's protecting me! I can hear her saying it already. I close my eyes and feel a breeze through the open window that smells like fresh-cut grass. I can hear a man calling for someone; I can't tell what he's saying, maybe he's just calling his cat, or maybe he's lost someone he loves. The thought makes my eyes water and spill tears.

"I'll see you tomorrow," my mother says. She leaves, not trying to fool the creaking stairs on her way out the door this time.

"Well, we did it!" Charles says. He folds me against him.

Pressing my face against his chest, I find it odd, right then, that the whole reason I met Charles was through losing my balance, an unforgivable sin in my family—and I wonder if this happy accident has cursed us, as if my genes won't let me have love without grace.

I'm about to go after my mother and have the argument we

should have had, about trust and responsibility, right in the front yard; I'm about to say that none of this is her business, I'm about to bring up the Vegas photograph, when Nellie hitch-glides into the room, her nightgown transparent and wrinkled against her blue-white skin, her nipples twin teardrops, dark faces under the fabric. Her pin-curled hair sprouts white wisps here and there, and her eyes look sleepy and childlike. She sees Charles and frowns, waving the vision of him away in a tiny, perfect *port de bras.* Then she sees me, standing like a Roman in my bedsheet, a look of proclamation on my face, and smiles. Her stomach growls, and she brings a hand to her belly, as if to settle it. Her lips press together and release; she breathes quickly through her nose. "Brrr. Brrr," she says.

"What is it?" Charles and I both ask at the same time.

"Bread," Nellie says. And then she offers her arm to be helped downstairs to the kitchen, where she will wait to be served.

I take after my father, who looks a lot like Rodolpho, tall and dark haired and naturally graceful, with a walk that flows from his hips. My father's name is Randall. He is a lawyer but not like the ones on TV. He does wills and trusts and house closings, mostly, and he works in a quiet, paneled office on Sycamore Street with brown carpeting and two cream-curtained windows and a secretary named Sue, with whom he went to high school. My mother works there, too. She helps him prepare and file documents. They met at church, presumably after my mother had come back from Vegas and was trying fitfully to ease back into her life here. She was serving drinks at the Black Cat, considered the raciest bar in town at that time (why, I don't know; they never had a gig more exciting than a beautiful black jazz singer named Talula Bell, who reportedly wore low-cut dresses). My father fell in love with her at the Women's Bible Study pastry table and convinced her to marry him after about a year, a woman he considered dangerous and mysterious. He encouraged her to go back to school. He's so gentle he can look at me and make me cry.

Which is what I'm doing now, sitting in his office across the desk from him. How I wish for Nellie's dusty velvet settee, her cracked walls, her cool canning basement! My stomach sits low in my hips, a rock. I couldn't even manage a *ronde de jamb,* the way I feel now. My mother planned not to be here when I came for the money, I'm sure.

My father brings me a cup of water from the cooler. "You know," he says. "In a few years, the age difference between you and the baker won't be such a big deal."

"His name is Charles!" I snap and immediately feel guilty. My father spreads his fingers and folds them together again, a concession. "Do you think I should wait?" I ask, even though I think I know what his answer is.

"If he loves you, he should wait for you," my father says, surprising me of course, his voice so warm, so forgiving that I can feel it on my skin. I let my head fall onto my folded arms. An expert on waiting, he brings me a dampened paper napkin to press to my forehead and sits with me until I am ready to go.

The next night at Nellie's house, I can't sleep. Maybe it's because my mother's downstairs on the fold-out couch—she said I can do what I want, but she's not letting a man who's not our relative stay in Nellie's house without her supervision. But Charles is happy to stay at his own apartment anyway because he says he wants to do everything right from here on out. He wants me to ask my parents if they'll have him over some evening so he can formally ask for my hand.

By midnight I can't take it anymore. I sneak past my mother and ride my bike downtown, past the high school, across the railroad tracks, past my father's office, past the bakery. I am a moving whisper, threading the soft air. I turn right on Elm Street, and as I slow in front of Charles's brick apartment building, I sling one leg in front of me and the other in back, imitating a sailing *jeté*. I have with me an extra pair of shorts and the cashier's check of my parents' college savings. I imagine my parents placing one dollar at a time into a pan and baking them lovingly. I walk the bike to his stoop, and I swear I can smell bread in the air around his front door.

It takes a long time for Charles to come after I knock. "You snuck out?" he asks, flush-faced and sleepy. He hasn't pushed open the screen to let me in. I've only been here a few times, right at the beginning, when we were so in love I thought we would never have to eat again or worry about being cold. I lost my virginity in his bedroom; I feel in some way I will always be in that room, remembering his hands gentle under my back, pushing into me a little bit at a time and then pulling back, until it felt good. He told me he'd been with two other women, one he dated through college, and one he'd broken up with right before he met me because she didn't want to marry him. "You get to a point," he'd said, "where if you can't have everything, you don't want anything."

I open the screen door myself and step inside. "I'm ready to go," I say. I can't figure out why my leg muscles are quivering and my skin feels feverish, bruised, as if I've ridden very hard. I didn't think I was rushing.

Charles rubs his hands back and forth through his hair. "Where?"

"Cincinnati," I say. "To get married." I think of Rodolpho's illicit loves in "Cin-cinn," as he called it, and I feel honored to follow in his perfectly measured footsteps.

Charles doesn't say anything just yet. But when he reaches for my hands, I know. "I want to do this right," he says. "I want your parents' blessings. I want a huge cake."

I shake my head. "It's now or never," I say. Something in me is sailing toward the ceiling, looking down at Charles and me, my bowed head, Charles's regretful face. I hear myself say, "You love me. You said so." I am shrinking to a child's body; I am bread with no yeast, a dancer with no spine.

"Maybe you need some time," he says. "Maybe you should think about it." He pulls me against him, and I can feel the rise and fall of his chest, a powdery film of flour on his neck, which sticks to my forehead. I think of what my father said, how if he loves me, he should wait. But then, if he loves me, shouldn't he do what I want? I can't wake up from what is happening.

I step away from him, and he lets me go. He lets me open the screen and walk outside, down the walk, to my bike. On the stage, he would have stopped me by now; we would begin a new *pas de deux*. Instead, I am on my bike again, thinking of how I am going to keep calm when I run into him again. I am shaking, my wheels wobbling as I ride back through town, to Nellie's house, finding my mother asleep on the sofa bed. She's curled in a ball in the center of the thin mattress, dreaming of court filings or maybe of Vegas or maybe of my father and me.

What if I only had one word to describe how I feel right now? I sit on the edge of the mattress and wait for my mother to wake up. Right then I can tell she will look like Nellie one day, her small features crowding toward the middle of her round face, and I will look like my father, pressing cool rags to her forehead with long fingers. My mother opens her eyes, and I think of it: dough. I'm aching to be transformed. My mother shifts on the mattress to make room for me, opens her arms. I lie down beside her and watch the leaf-laced moonlight move across the wall, waiting for sleep the way some people wait for love.

Lennie Remembers the Angels

Lately, she's going back to the two tall sisters in their white choir robes standing next to the box she put her mother in, looking at her, not like somebody you pass on the street, but staring *into* her, eyes marching right inside her like she's just a house with the doors flung wide open. The two of them like any other woman in her church, wide-shouldered and big-busted, black hair and honey-brown skin shining, the way she'd look someday, she thought then. The women stood there while Reverend Earl was preaching by the grave, robe hems lifting in the hot air, moving like someone sighing, only no one heard them and no one saw them. And it wasn't no dream. It was what happened, Lennie holding the paper bag one of the women had handed her, the bag gone soft and furry with the sweat of her hand, a bag full of cash, which she used to pay for the box and then the hole in the clay and some flowers, too, even though her uncle, her mother's own brother, said her mother didn't deserve flowers. *A whore like her.*

Storm coming up now, air heavy on her forehead. She rolls over, pulls a pillow to her chest out of habit so she won't feel the flatness, the breasts gone and now just bone and ribbed, scarred skin. She rocks and cradles the pillow and tries to remember what the women were telling her without moving their red lips, that everything was going to be fine, she had her whole life ahead of her, the past didn't matter. This was what she knew she'd heard that day, and she'd believed it. She was sixteen, small for her age, small like a child, and men loved that about her, the way they could put their hands around her waist and touch their thumbs and middle fingers without squeezing. Only they did squeeze.

The first crack lights up the room, everything bone white and then black, even though it's only late afternoon. Another thump like it's in her own walls, and she's on her feet, down the short hall, past the row of Cedric's school pictures, past the State Farm calendar, finding the ashtray and cigarettes on the coffee table in the front room. The rain starts, fat, slapping drops. Another thump and she screams. "Gimme that fucking lighter," she commands the room, and then she sees its metal tip glinting next to the stove; she had used it earlier to light the gas, she remembers now. She lights her cigarette on the third try and stands by the kitchen window, shaking and watching the storm mix up the trees.

Another thump and she pounds the counter to keep her fear and her rage at the fear, after all this time, in the bottom of her throat where it belongs. Then she sees what's making the sound, not really the storm but a little man coming out of the apartment next door, screen slapping the outside wall as he hurries down the back steps and tugs at a mattress in the backseat of a long, green Chevrolet. His skinny body jerks back and forth as he pulls, shaking his head to get the rain out of his eyes. She wonders how he can reach the pedals in a car like that. Finally, the mattress gives and one corner splashes into a puddle before he can stop it. Lennie puts a hand over her mouth because she feels like laughing, but she knows it isn't right.

She watches him stagger as he pulls the mattress to his shoulder and makes his way back to the door, rain rolling down the bedding like the side of a roof. She steps back from the window, even though she knows he won't see her. He's Asian; she can't tell what kind. The last family that lived next door was Vietnamese—four kids and so noisy she prayed they'd be deported. She heard they got evicted for cutting a hole in the floor and using the basement for a toilet. She doesn't know if this is true, but it did take four months to get anyone new in there and a lot of people looking at it. Meantime, she had gotten used to the quiet.

The man makes one more trip to the Chevrolet and comes back with two bulging garbage bags. He grimaces against the rain. "You go on and make a face," Lennie whispers to him. "Ain' no one want you here anyway."

Sometime during the night, the storm clears and the claws unhook themselves from Lennie's stomach. She wakes up on the couch, the sun already high and sucking the blue out of the sky. Another hot day. Sunday. Her birthday. She sits up, presses her fingers to her forehead and thinks of fifty years. Born May 5, 1950. Five-five-fifty-fifty. Some numerology type would get all over that. "Maybe this my year," Lennie says, pushing herself to her feet. She makes coffee, scrambles an egg, toasts and butters some white bread. She eats at the kitchen sink, gazing at the trees lining the gravel parking lot, their leaves glossy and deep green, still wet and heavy from the storm. She thinks about propping her door open to catch a breeze, then thinks better of it. Then she's glad she waited because the little man comes out the back door, walking fast, screen clapping against the outside wall again. Her wall. She'll have to talk to him about that. He rolls down his car window and backs out, and she gets a good look at his face as he turns his head to see behind him. He's older than she thought, maybe fifty, maybe older than that. Hard to tell with men, with Asian men especially.

Lennie finishes her breakfast, showers, and dresses for church. As she pulls her hair scarf from her purse and checks the lock on her back door, she sees the green Chevrolet; the man is already back from wherever he went. She goes out the front door, squinting in the sun, locks up, and starts down her steps.

"Hello."

Lennie hears the voice and the accent and knows it's her neighbor before she turns to see him standing at his open front door. He is smiling, nodding at her as if they're already friends having a pleasant little conversation. *Small talk is for small people,* Lennie thinks. Who had said that to her once? She presses out a closed-mouth smile. "Hello," she says.

The man steps onto his stoop, and Lennie steps off her last step into the warm, wet grass. He sees this and stops, puts a hand to his chest. "Duc Li." The sound in "Duc" is something between "oo" and "uh."

"Duke?" Lennie says.

"Duc Li," the man says again, nodding.

"Duck," Lennie says.

"Yes," the man says, although Lennie knows she wasn't even close. *Why do those people have to talk up in their nose like that?* she wonders.

"And, you, name?" Duc Li says, the last word swinging up in his throat as if he's just remembered he's asking a question.

"Lennie," she says. She takes another step away from him, wet grass brushing her ankles and marking her hose. *They need to take a mower to this place,* she thinks. She sees her bus turning the corner. "Nice to meet you," she says, although this isn't true, it isn't nice, but she doesn't want to miss her bus.

Lennie walks quickly to the curb, watching the bus, which is waiting to make a left turn onto her street. She hears Duc Li sing out, "And you!" in a thin, reedy voice that sounds like a sick child's. She throws her arm up in a quick wave but doesn't turn around.

This isn't the church she went to as a child, where her mother was buried. That church burned down while she was in Atlanta trying to get clean, her small son left with her Aunt Olivia, who was actually her mother's aunt. She heard they moved the bodies before they built the shopping center, but her mother's grave never had a marker except a few stones, so Lennie figures she's still in the old churchyard, under all that concrete, where it's cool and quiet and no one can bother her.

The church Lennie goes to now is beige brick with thick beige carpet and long, blond-wood pews, a far cry from the splintered folding chairs that cut into the back of your thighs and nothing but packed dirt for a floor. And no organ, not even a piano. And no air-conditioning. When she went to that church, all she could think about was getting out, first so she could play with her girlfriends and later so she could get with the boys who were turning into men, who couldn't be made to go to church anymore, and if they did, they sat in the back so she felt their eyes moving over her neck and arms like a slow fire.

Today the sermon is about Jesus turning the water into wine, and Lennie thinks of when she joined twenty years ago, having just come back from AA in Atlanta, still shaky, her son ten years old and not sure who she was. The preacher is saying the wine is a symbol for something else. Lennie sits up straighter in her pew to see where he goes with this. He says the wine is a sign for the joy of life.

"Not that you got to drink it to be happy," he says, and people laugh. He's young, round-faced. Most of the brothers and sisters are gray-headed.

A woman moans an Amen to Lennie's left. She doesn't think this preacher is going to last—he'll go on to bigger churches that put their services on TV—but his hoarse, microphoned words make her think of other signs: her mother's death a sign of sin's punishment, her own burning house a sign for starting over, her breasts cut away a sign that she would no longer be the woman she was.

The preacher's asking people for prayer dedications. Over the years, Lennie always called out her mother's name, Celia, because it's true, she was a whore, at least for one man, who kept her in drugs until he got tired of her, then beat her unconscious one night and dragged her into the road and drove back and forth over her until she was in pieces. Broke Lennie's father's heart in pieces, too, because he died soon after that. If she'd had a daughter, Lennie would have named her Celia and raised her to become the kind of woman her mother might have been, if things had been different. Instead, she had Cedric, and then she left him when he was only four and didn't come back until he was ten, and then he looked her in the face and said his mother was dead.

Pray for me, Lennie wants to say. But nobody ever asks for that. So she doesn't, either.

On the bus home, she thinks about taking a trip, maybe to the ocean, which she has been to once, when she was a child. It was before her father's heart attack, the one that put a scar up his middle and the end to his working. It was before her mother left them for Dag, who always had money and rings, thick gold on every finger. Lennie remembers not believing her father when he said they were going to the beach because the ocean in her mind was so clean and blue, she didn't think whites would let coloreds near it.

But they did drive to the beach, right onto it even, sand stinging her arm where it hung over the side of the car through the open back window, sand spraying the wheel wells like rain on their tin roof at home, sand flying in the windows, sticking in her teeth. She collected the grains with her tongue and swallowed them and thought about where'd they'd been, where they'd had to travel to land in her belly. In the water, she opened her mouth to the warm, salty wet, closed her eyes, let wave after wave roll her body into the surf, water rushing in her ears, drowning out her father's warning calls and sounding like somewhere she'd been before. And the most amazing sight: chocolate and coffee and caramel skins of other children, of men and women, shining wet in the light that came from every direction, everyone laughing and walking as if this was all there was—sun, water, sand, and brown people in their own paradise.

The bus chokes to a stop at the curb in front of Lennie's apartment building. She takes her time getting off, crossing the street and the lawn, glancing at the apartment next to hers, trying to judge if her new neighbor is watching. She doesn't want to try to make conversation. Inside, she splashes water on her face, changes clothes, waits to check the red light on the answering machine in the small bedroom until she has nothing left to do.

The light is blinking. She holds her finger just above the button, listening, as if she might be able to tell the voice before it starts. There are words and then there are the words behind the words, her father used to say, especially when she started staying out late with men, and he sat up waiting and watching for her, knowing that getting angry would've done nothing but drive her away, like it did her mother. What did he think of women, how they left him when he was too weak to even argue?

Cedric. Like she hoped. "Mama, Nina and me wanna come over and take you to lunch, OK? Maybe over to Herbie's. Guess you at church. Call me."

So nice to be called. So right. She walks through her house and inspects it, straightens a rug, smoothes the bedspread. Opens all the curtains. She spritzes the couch pillows with her favorite perfume, sits down and lights a cigarette, watches the bluish ribbon rise and spread and curl like a storm cloud, like a woman's hair, loose and flowing, underwater. She thinks of her little girl's braids standing around her head for the seconds she could stay under the waves, all that water and deep around her and she wasn't even scared. She walks back down the hall to call Cedric, who's a good son even though he's had his share of turnaround changes, and as she dials, she thinks she might look into a bus ticket to the coast. Maybe Myrtle Beach.

Answering machine. Probably they're outside with Nina's kids. She tells them she'd love to go to Herbie's. "Hi, Sally," she says to Nina's older daughter. "Hi, Lola."

She hangs up, stubs out the cigarette, changes back into the dress she wore to church, and smiles at herself in the bathroom mirror, even though she's feeling the first ache of worry in the soft space between her ribs, the way she feels when the clouds gather over the development down the hill and lightning winks behind the trees. She can hear the man moving around in the apartment next door, rustling like a small animal behind the walls. Then she hears his back door open, and she steps to the side of her window, where she can see. He leans out with two plants, pink impatiens and some kind of a cactus, both in green plastic pots with the price stickers still on. He leaves them on the stoop, proof he's there to stay.

She stretches out on the couch, balancing her feet on the arm. Passing cars sigh on the road, and she thinks of the two women in their choir robes, the air around them alive some-how, looking at her in a way that moved through her, telling her: *You gonna be OK.* But asking, too. She thinks of her job at the nursing home, turning all those poor bony bodies, won-dering who will turn her someday.

"Stop it," Lennie says to the air, and right after that, she falls asleep.

When she wakes up, it's nearly five o'clock, sun in her eyes. She knows it's late without checking; she could always tell time within ten minutes by the light, the way her father taught her. But she looks anyway at the black lines on the clock, and she walks slowly to the smaller bedroom, her hips stiff, to check the answering machine, knowing she wouldn't have slept through any rings.

Red light steady as a stare. "Fine," Lennie says to the room, to the dust floating in the sunlight. "Fine."

She smoothes her hair, finds her purse and keys, heads for the bus stop on the curb before remembering Sunday bus ser-vice cuts off at five. She decides to walk to the Kentucky Fried Chicken a half mile down Church Street next to the gas sta-tion. She'll take herself out to dinner and pick up some ciga-rettes, too.

She's stepping off the curb, checking to make sure she's remembered her wallet, starting to cross the street, feeling around in her purse, looking down, and then there is a metal flash and sound so great she can't tell the two apart, and she feels not pain, really, but weight, like the waves rolling her down into heavy sand, and she can't tell where her body is, and then there is nothing.

Someone is crying. Lennie tries to comfort her, but the more she tries, the louder the moans.

"You steal," a voice says, right above her head somewhere.

"No," Lennie says. She's done a lot of things in her life, but she never took anything that wasn't hers.

"Steal!"

She tries to respond, but she is too tired, and it's too bright to open her eyes.

"No! No move!"

"Oh my god," a woman's voice says. A voice she recognizes.

She hears scraping footsteps near her head, fading, then returning. And her back and arms are hot, so she tries to roll on her side, but someone gently pushes her back. "Goddamn you," she mutters, and she opens her eyes and there is a face above hers, a boy's face she thinks, but the sun is behind it. *Cedric?* she thinks or maybe says. Then she's being lifted, and the pain moves through her like a wedge of hot metal from her leg to her shoulder, and then she passes out.

There's no reason to be confused, she keeps telling herself every time she opens her eyes, sometimes when a nurse comes in to check on her, to change one of the bags dripping clear liquid into her arm. But she is. Once she sees herself tearing out the needle and getting up to leave, but when she looks again, it's still there, and she doesn't know whether it was a dream or not.

Then she thinks it's her breasts again, the doctors telling

her they were poisoning her body and they would have to take them. She laughs at the word *take,* like they're children she can't control, like they can be brought back once they learn to behave. But then she looks down at her chest, and it's as flat as a girl's, the white gown like a field of snow, like the choir robes the angels wore. Well, they were angels, weren't they? Meeting her in front of the church like that, and she only had five dollars in her pocket, wasn't even enough to have the hole dug. They handed her a paper bag, twisted tight at the mouth like a wino's sack, only it was so light it felt like there was nothing in it. They handed her that sack and walked away, leaving her in the dirt churchyard like this was the kind of thing people did every day.

How did she know to walk to the back of the church and find Sarylee, the secretary, and dump that sack all over a chair? Money falling out and tumbling to the floor, damp and folded. Almost five hundred dollars. She had always said she'd remember the exact number forever because that would be her lucky number for the rest of her life, but then she'd forgotten it right away, almost as soon as the money was spent. Enough for the hole and the preacher and a pine coffin. And flowers, too. And even some left over, which she had promised herself she would put down on a gravestone, a big white marble one, but then she'd spent it on a dress for getting married to Tony, and it was that dress she wanted to save when she woke up one night in that drafty country house he stuck her in, the fire heat holding her down on the bed, its sound like people whispering, laughing. She thought of the dress even before her own son.

It was lightning that started it, turned that house to black bones, as if to say, *This is your heart, this is what it looks like.* She wants to get on her knees and pray about it, even now, but she can't move, can't even think of how she would bend to kneel.

Then there is the policeman, his chest a gray wall, the loose pink skin of his neck wagging as he asks her what she remembers. She remembers a lot of things, things she'd rather forget, and here they are lined up in front of her like Judgment Day. The policeman asks if she can tell him anything about the car.

"The car?" she asks, her throat surprised at its sound.

"That hit you?" Metal pin tapping a clipboard. Clock hands clicking in their circle. Ticking her to sleep.

"You got a nice young man here to see you," the nurse says. "You gonna be fine."

"Who?" Lennie says. Then she sees her son in the doorway, looking at her with a smile that says he'd rather be somewhere else. His church smile. His good son smile. The one that seems to hurt him from the way he squints. Shifting from one foot to the other.

"Hi, Mama," he says. "How you feeling?" He jingles some change in his pocket.

"She a lot better, ain't she," the nurse says to Lennie. She wheels a chair to the side of the bed and presses a button to push Lennie upright. Lennie can feel her insides folding hotly as she rises.

"No," she moans.

The nurse peels back the covers. "Gotta start somewhere," she says. "You gonna be OK."

Home. Right leg broken, five broken ribs—two on the left and three on the right. Contusions on the left shoulder. *Upper extremities,* they called it. Where she threw herself against the door of her burning house. Where she burped her son. Now she can't even think about lifting that arm. The car hit her leg first, then flipped her over the hood onto her shoulder. Then left her to die. The worst part: scrubbing the asphalt from her skin, the palms of her hands where she had evidently tried to break her fall. She had cried like a child during that.

Nurse coming twice a day. Aqua-blue uniform, skin so white it's almost blue, too. Nora. Wears her hair in a ponytail with a rubber band and no makeup. No wedding ring, either. Lennie wants to tell her she could fix herself up a little, probably find herself someone, but then what does she have to say about men? Chasing after Tony with his almond eyes and the muscles in his shoulders like something molded, not flesh, two teardrops that slid from his neck and fanned over her in bed, how she loved his size. She loved men who towered over her, and most did, but she loved the biggest, the ones who made her feel like a little doll. Thinking of him, if she lets herself go into that first year, the year Cedric was born, can still make her thighs twitch and tighten with the heat. That year, before his drinking set his anger on fire, before he started accusing her, asking her to prove that was really his son, and how could she do that? It was him who was cheating, and she started drinking too because it was something they had in common and because sometimes when he was drunk he got slow and soft, usually after he'd gotten paid and the money stretched out in front of them like a long velvet cushion until Tuesday of the following week, when there were only beans or those yellow noodles in the crinkly sacks to eat. That first year, they lived in that country shack of a house with nothing, and he was happy she was pregnant, telling her she was so beautiful. That first summer, the fireflies were thick in the trees, and some nights when it was too hot in the house, they laid down in the grass and made love with crickets srilling all around.

One time she looked up, past the blue-black sheen of Tony's hair, past the swell of his back and the twin slopes of her drawn-up knees and saw a plane sliding silently across the sky. She had never been in a plane and had always wanted to, but that night she felt sorry for the people inside, that they could not know the pleasure that ran down to her very fingertips, so much of it she thought she could die right then, never even get to see her baby, and be happy enough to let go of it all.

Nora sponges her down in the morning and helps her dress and eat. This morning Lennie's in her recliner in a slip and underpants. A nylon bandage buckled around her ribs like the tightest girdle she's ever had. The hospital doctor told her Medicaid would cover fake breasts to put in her bra, but she said no. Who is she going to impress?

"Which one?" Nora asks, holding up two dresses, one red with white flowers and one a yellow check. Lennie looks at them but doesn't see them yet; she's not quite ready to get up off that dewy grass, to give up all that roundness—her breasts and belly, Tony's buttocks and the tip of his purple-brown penis.

"Ms. Williams?"

Lennie sighs, lets go. "I don't care."

Nora hugs the dresses to her like limp children. She cocks her head to one side like a schoolteacher. "Ms. Williams, would you like me to help you do your makeup today?"

"What for? Huh? Where am I going?" Lennie asks. The itch under her leg cast is hot sandpaper on her skin. She claws it anyway, knowing it won't help. She doesn't know why she likes being rude to Nora. Maybe because she will take it; she'll just be more and more polite until she freezes in place, all that blue skin and pale-brown hair still as death.

Nora gives up. "OK, the yellow one." Lennie lets her arms

go slack, and Nora gently lifts the hurt one first, her fingertips like cold little stones, then the other. Then she helps Lennie stand so that the dress falls down her back, and Lennie buttons it herself.

Nora sits down on the couch across from her. "Are you sure there isn't anything more I can do for you?"

"Don't you have your next appointment?"

"You know, it's OK to take help right now. You need to let people take care of you until you're better."

Lennie tries to lean forward in her chair, but the pain stops her. She grunts out her words, using her best white talk to try to get through to the woman. "For your information, my son is coming over in a while. I am not some charity case. You look at me and you think you know what you see. But you don't know anything."

Nora's lips get straight and thin; Lennie can see she's made her point. Nora stands, gathers her brown purse and her white notebook. "See you tomorrow, Ms. Williams."

Front door pulls closed, and Lennie sighs. She nods to her father's picture on the wall, next to it her parents' wedding picture in front of the courthouse, her mother wearing a stiff white dress with lace at the wrists and throat, looking serious, her father in a dark suit, sweat shining on his high forehead, smiling. Their features narrow and spare. She wishes she could step into that picture and touch their soft faces and warn them about everything, tell them they can save themselves. But what about her? She doesn't even have a picture of Tony—all that floated into the air the night of the fire—and after that they moved in with his parents since hers were already dead, and he was never there, and when he was there he hit her or sometimes they drank together until she couldn't even wake up when her son was crying. And then she left

Cedric, left him with those brown stick arms wrapped around her aunt's leg, his shoulders capped with those teardrops of muscle just like his father's, except small and nowhere near as strong.

Maybe an hour passes, her just thinking, waiting for Cedric to come, until she's sure he won't come, and she starts crying, thinking of that day two weeks ago in the church when she wanted to ask everyone to pray for her. "Please," she says into the quiet. "Please."

The knock wakes her, and the pain comes first to certain places, and then everywhere at once. "Mama, it's me, open up."

She has to unlock it herself. "OK," she tries to say, but she can barely whisper with the effort of pulling herself onto the crutches. She crab-steps past the coffee table, then leans against the back door as she turns the lock. She sees her son's sagging white truck next to her neighbor's Chevrolet and wonders why she hasn't heard the little man lately. She steps away from the door. "You can open it now."

Cedric steps in, and she's hit with the smell of him—sweat and cologne and smoke. He follows her slowly back into the living room. She tries to sense his mood while he's still behind her—she's always been able to tell more about a person if she closes her eyes and listens to them. She can tell he's tired, maybe worried about something, from the way his feet shuffle and his breath comes out too fast from his nose. "Help me back down in this chair," she says and winces as he grabs her too strongly and lowers her. "Now, there's a tall bottle of white pills and a smaller bottle of blue pills on the sink in there," she says, pointing at the bathroom. He comes back with the pills, and she doesn't bother to ask for water; she just swallows them as quickly as she can, waiting for the slicing pain in her arm and leg and ribs to subside. He puts them back in the bathroom.

"Mama, you don't look too good."

"Thanks, Cedric."

"No, I mean it. They feeding you?"

"Yes, they feed me nasty crap and I eat it. Got me a white nurse who don't know how to fix her own hair, not to mention mine."

This makes Cedric laugh. He slaps his knee and falls back against her couch cushion. "Mama, you a mess." And Lennie feels a warmth that starts in her chest and spreads into her neck and then her face. Her son, a grown man right in front of her, laughing with his wide mouth that turns up at the corners just like his father's. *I made you,* she thinks. She smiles. She goes through the things she won't ask, like where he's working now, or if he's working, or whether he's talked to his father lately. "How's Nina and Sally?"

"They fine, they fine. Listen, I got news for you." Cedric's face looks serious, and Lennie pulls in her breath to steady herself. The pain medication is flowing over her, and she knows she can live with it if he's going to ask her for money again because he's alive, and as long as he's alive, she is, too. Cedric sits forward, folds his long fingers. "Nina gonna have a baby."

"You?" is all Lennie manages to say, and then she flings her arms out to him, never mind the stab in her shoulder, and Cedric comes around the coffee table to her and kneels between her cast and her good leg and she pulls him to her and rocks him like she used to do when they laid awake in that leaky house, listening to the rain splashing in all their pots and pans. She can already see the baby, slick from just being born, being handed to her, and it will be light-skinned like Nina but wiry like Cedric. She can hear its thin mewling, oh and see the head turning, rooting for milk. She knows she will be there.

Cedric pulls away and sits back on his heels, looking down to check the beeping pager clipped to the waistband of his baggy shorts. The bands of muscles in his arms roll over each other, and Lennie allows herself to think of Tony, how he kneeled, asking her to marry him, except he almost fell over because he was so drunk, and they both laughed because they were so young, and it was so, so funny. They were young and black and poor and the world had nothing to give them, but it didn't matter because they didn't need anything then; they would have laughed like hyenas at anyone who thought they were good enough to pity them.

Cedric's on his feet. "Let me use your phone, Mama." While he's down the hall, Lennie is listing all the questions she has to ask, but when he comes back, he's jingling his keys. "I gotta go."

"Wait, now," Lennie says. "You gotta tell me more! When's it due?"

Cedric's shifting his feet now, finding the right key. "I don't know. Nina just took a home test."

"She going to the doctor, ain' she?"

"I guess so. Look, Mama, I gotta go."

Lennie wants to get to her feet but can't. "Was that her calling?"

"No." Cedric bends to kiss her cheek. His lips are dry, quick. "You want me to bring you some dinner?"

"OK, if you can." Lennie tries to act as if it doesn't matter either way, but she's hopeful.

"You want some fried chicken?"

Lennie gets her purse from under the recliner, hands him a

twenty. "Why don't you get some for yourselves too and bring Nina and Sally over?"

Cedric smiling, pushes the bill into his running shorts. "OK then." Then he's out the door, and all that's left is his smell and the heat from where he was standing.

Lennie closes her eyes, thinks about the baby, which is carrying a little bit of her inside it, unfurling inside Nina. She liked Nina before; now maybe she can love her. She lets herself slide into a light sleep. Then she's seeing the women by her mother's grave, telling her she would be OK, meaning there would be a day when all the pain she had felt and made for herself would somehow come to something good, and on that day she'd find her way to something like grace. She drifts on this, waves swelling underneath and lifting her salty body to the sun, and she is sleeping lightly when there's another knock on her door. She opens her eyes and listens. "Cedric, that you?"

"Hello," a man's voice says but not Cedric's, thinner.

"Who is it?" Reaching for the crowbar she put under her chair, next to her purse.

"Duc Li. Next door?" That swinging upward at the end of his voice, like he's always surprised.

Lennie lets the air out of her chest. If not Cedric, then at least it's someone to help her pass the time. "Come in."

She hears her screen slap, and she wants to ask this man if anyone ever explained to him about not letting doors slam. He comes into the living room where she can see him, and he's holding something white in both hands. She squints to see it better. It seems too dark all of a sudden—did she sleep later than she thought? He bends and places the bundle on the table, and then she can see it's a package of candles, bound in twine. He points toward the ceiling. "Stome tonight," he says.

"What?" Then she understands. Storm. And as soon as she understands the word, she's looking out the front window down the hill toward the development, where the weather always comes in, and even though the sun is still shining on the street, the sky down there is a bruised gray. Her chest gets tight again. She can hear the air moving in and out of her lungs, feel the gathering pressure at her temples. Duc Li is watching her. He is so short that he only has to bend a little to get to her eye level. "You OK?" Words halting, like a waterbug zigzagging.

Lennie nods. "Thanks for the candles."

"In case the lights go—" He makes a slicing gesture with his hands. "Bad," he says, shaking his head. Lennie looks at the clock. Two hours since Cedric left. She thinks about calling about dinner but doesn't want to beg. She's too old for that. He said he was coming back. He's a man now, and his word has to count for something.

Duc Li is cutting open the package with a pocketknife. "You want?" he says, miming putting a candle in a holder.

Lennie shakes her head. "I don't have any."

"OK," Duc Li says, smiling. "OK." He holds up one finger signaling her to wait and goes out the back door, screen slamming, making her jump.

"Goddamnit!" Lennie yells at him. She's hungry, her son isn't going to show up—she knows this even if she wants to pretend otherwise—and the sky is going to crack open any minute. Truth is, after the fire, she never liked candles. She keeps a flashlight by her bed but didn't think to put it in reach since the accident.

Duc Li comes back with a roll of foil. He tears a piece and makes a mound of it and presses the base of one candle into it. Then he makes another. Lennie doesn't try to stop him. "You see?" he says, and Lennie nods. She sees. She's going to sit in this apartment alone, waiting out the storm, hoping the lightning doesn't burn her alive like it almost did the last time. She's going to sit here until her body knits itself together again, and then she'll go back to work, and when she can't work anymore, she'll go back to sitting again, and then she'll die alone. Yes, she sees.

"I made," Duc Li says, pointing to the candles. "Carter Candle Factory." Except he says it "Carteh Cander Fahctree." Lennie wants to laugh at him for his cartoon talk and jerky gestures, the comical grin on his face. She wants to laugh at him for thinking this country would be so much better for him, that he'd ever belong here. But then the first thunder hits, and she hears it pushing through the air almost before it explodes into sound, but she can't stop the yelp that tears itself out of her throat.

Duc Li steps back, and for some reason she sees no point in not telling him the situation. "I'm scared. Storm," she says, pointing at the ceiling like Duc Li did and feeling ridiculous. "Can you get my pills?" She points to the bathroom.

He brings them, sets them on the table beside her. "You stay steel," he says and goes out the back door again, and she keeps hearing the word "steel." She knows he means "still." But where did she hear it before? She closes her eyes and what she sees is a boy's face—maybe a man's—looking down at her, sun behind him so she can't make out the features. She's on her back and the pavement's burning her, and she's thinking someone's accusing her of stealing. Then she realizes he's the one who found her. He saw her get hit.

Duc Li comes back with two bowls of steaming rice and vegetables, one fork, one set of chopsticks. "Here," he says, holding one out to her.

"No, that's OK," she says. "I'm not hungry." She isn't. She's angry—at her fear of mere weather, the picture of Duc Li standing over her in the street, the stupidity of not seeing the car coming, the pain that's coming back. Duc Li places the bowl on her coffee table. She reaches for the two bottles of pills, the pills rattling like ice in a glass, all those glasses of gin she drank, toward the end with no ice at all. No glass even. She opens the tall bottle and finds that most of the pills are gone. A lot more than earlier today. Cedric. Always nipping a little here, a little there. She squeezes the bottle and shakes her head. Tears dripping off her nose. What did she expect?

Duc Li takes the bottle from her. He reads the label, counts out one white pill, two blue pills. He takes a glass from the drainer in the kitchen, fills it with water from the tap, hands her the glass and the pills. He sits on his heels near where her son was sitting just hours before, telling her about a baby, filling her with hope even as he was stealing from her. Duc Li takes the glass from her and offers her the bowl. "You eat." She shakes her head, but he leans forward and pushes the bowl into her hands. "Eat," he says. He sits back on his heels again, prepared to wait.

Lightning now, turning his face gray, then darkening it. No more sun on the street, just the heavy air, the waiting stillness. She holds the warm bowl, holds her breath, listening for thunder. Duc Li picks up his bowl and begins to eat. His fingers are narrow and long, like a woman's, his chopsticks click lightly against the bowl. The thunder rolls into the room, and he looks up at her, smiles while she grips the chair arm with her free hand, bearing down on the urge to scream. Alone, she could let it out into a pillow but not with him here. *Do you think this is funny?* Lennie wants to ask him. *Me, trapped here with you?* But Duc Li is back to shoveling in mouthfuls of food. He is almost finished by the time Lennie manages the first bite. The rice is sticky and warm, and the vegetables, bell pepper and snow peas, crunch loud like the thud of blood in her ears. She keeps going until her bowl is empty. Duc Li takes it, stacks it into his own. "Thank you," she says. He nods, rises fluidly to his feet, heads for the back door.

"Wait a minute," she says. "Do you remember my name?"

Duc Li seems to think this is funny. "Len-nie," he says with a pause in the middle. "Like my wife. Li Ni." No smile now.

"Where is she?"

"Gone. Long time."

Lennie doesn't say anything to this. The medicine is loosening her muscles, relaxing her jaw. She barely twitches at the next roll of thunder. The room is almost dark; normally she would turn off all the lights and unplug her radio and television and smoke cigarettes until the worst had passed. Tonight she doesn't even have the energy to ask him to hand her the pack. He stands in the shadow of her doorway, waiting, she thinks, for her to say something, but she can't. She's thinking of her mother now, her broken body nailed into the pine box, how only a week before Dag killed her, her mother was standing on his rickety front porch yelling, 'You ain't my daughter! You get outta here, you little bitch!' The drugs had carved deep holes under her eyes and cheekbones. Lennie's thinking that's what death is, not being known. She's thinking of the quality of the brown sisters' voices, like breath over a bottle, telling her not to worry—weren't they saying she could one day live in grace? She lifts her hand, reaches, waits for it, the dry pressure of Duc Li's hand closing over hers.

Shed This Life

Today my belly popped out like a just-opened jelly lid, and now only my sweatpants fit. I figure I've been incognito for about four and a half months, but I'm small and I knew it couldn't last.

I get on the bus, and the driver, Mario, looks me over, which is what he normally does, except this time not because he wants me but because he can tell. "So you give it away, no?" he says, lip curling over the "o," eyes flicking to my bare ring finger, a smile that doesn't reach his eyes. I consider a knuckle jab to the throat, but there's a bus full of morning-faced commuters staring at me, college students, cleaning ladies, night watchmen trying to get home, and I can tell no one's going to support me on this.

I hand over the fare and walk all the way to the back of the bus. There's no place to sit, and no one offers me a place. This is what my mother was talking about when she complained about the sexual revolution. All it means is women put out with no respect and no security, she'd say every time the news flashed some new quip from Gloria Steinem, which seemed to be often because it was the seventies then and all my friends' parents were getting divorced. Except my parents, who died together in a car accident my senior year in high school and left me to figure out sex and its politics for myself.

The bus heaves forward, and somebody turns up a radio over the laboring engine, and it's tuned to a local call-in show where the host named Howie is saying it's time for a brand new country, one where people take responsibility for their actions. It's time, he says, to get back to a modicum of decency in this country. People who want free love in this country will find out they've made their bed and now it's time to lie down!

"You mean women," I mutter to Howie as I grab for a gray rubber loop and lean against a seat. My hip pokes the shoulder of a fat young man who turns his moon face up at me until I look down at him with an expression that says, *Fuck with me asshole, please.* He gets interested in his hands folded in his lap, and when the bus takes a corner, I lean into him harder and he just stares straight ahead. We're leaving Skokie and heading into the city, where I work for a dentist who bills himself as Dr. Tooth the Kiddie Dentist in the Yellow Pages. The skyline ahead is gray with the light behind it and looks like a cardboard cutout on a wide, flat stage. A pregnant woman sits on a bench, biting a hangnail, staring past us. A teenaged girl pushes a stroller slowly on the sidewalk. The world is full of swollen-bellied women, babies needing to be tended.

We stop in the last suburb before the city, and the night workers shuffle off and the day workers shuffle in, and then we start up again and I can smell the diesel and I want, for a moment, to throw up. Instead, I focus on the posters near the ceiling advertising diet shakes, candy bars, chewing gum, sugary drinks for kids—all of which help the dentist get richer and me keep my job, at least for a while. It's a tangled world. And something else: I'm carrying money. There's money in kids and everyone's on the bandwagon: politicians, advertisers, talk-show hosts. I imagine layers and layers of wet dollar bills thickening in my belly, pennies forming the dark weight of lungs, heart, brain. Someone predicted this—Gloria Steinem maybe, I don't know, because I was smart but not a great student and in general I just wasn't paying attention after my parents died, hoping things would get better when I wasn't looking, and that one day I would find a way to make them proud of me, showcasing my unique abilities once I figured out what they were.

I get to the dentist's office and settle behind the front desk with its high white counter and sliding-glass window. The game I play every day is to get in as quietly as I can so the dentist can't hear me and won't ask me to do anything. But when he comes out of his office, angry because he thinks I'm late, he sees me sitting there, pulling files for the day or stacking papers into neat piles like a newscaster, smirking at his red face so he knows I got him again. Gotcha, I try to say with my smirk. This is how I play with him because I wish I didn't need this job, because I know the dentist could fire me for no reason, and then I might be one of those women on the street watching the cars pass. I wish I were a billionaire. But then again, I want to be normal. I'm scared that if I really had money, I'd start playing golf and eating finger foods at country clubs and thinking it's necessary to fly to Bora Bora for the total eclipse of the sun. And maybe it's not necessary. Or maybe I'm just scared in general.

This morning when I hear the dentist's shoes squeaking up the hallway, I slide my chair as close to the counter as possible to hide my belly, a reflex.

"I need you to stay late tonight," he says. "I'm doing a seminar on infant dental hygiene at the Y." Normally he stays late on Thursdays so people can come in after work.

I don't answer. I am getting more and more annoyed with this day. Instead, I make myself stand up, press my fists into the small of my back, and lean into a yawn. The dentist looks down, takes in the bulge in my sweatpants, doesn't congratulate me. He says, "I hope when you have that child, you'll have enough sense to breastfeed it."

The word breast coming out of his pale mouth makes my ears cock as if I've heard a sound in the night. I look at the brochures he's stacking, pink and blue, with photos of young children with gingivitis and the title "Dental Care Starts in the Womb," and that makes me feel a little sick, imagining the dentist with his head between my legs and his scraper and polisher and suction tube humming, working on my baby, while I try to be still.

The dentist probably thinks I'm not smart enough to make good health decisions, seeing as how I'm working for him for minimum wage and only took one college course, philosophy 101. But who needs to go to college when the world is a wide-open place? I expected things would come up, and they did, but not the right things. Not yet.

I call the dentist's first patient, a little girl with blond ringlets framing bright-blue eyes. Her mother pushes her along from behind. The girl starts to cry as the door swings shut behind them. She steals a look back at me from between her mother's legs, and I think I see a distress signal flashing in her glassy eyes. Maybe she's trying to tell me she's not a little girl at all but an alien trapped on Earth, and this dental hygiene gig is a scam to poison her and no one will ever know her story. I almost get up and pull her into my arms, whisper how I know her secret and we are going to run away together to a place where no one can tell us what to do. But I just give her a reassuring smile instead. I turn the radio on to the classic-rock station and listen to the same ten Eagles songs all day.

On the bus home, I am even more pissed than earlier because I'm getting home late, because I didn't have time for lunch seeing as how the dentist was jamming through one rotten-toothed child after another, because none of my sexy short skirts and shimmery dress shirts fit anymore. And because I'll have to tell my boyfriend, Ted, who will be all for a baby, and this just complicates things. "No more free love," I say out loud, and the fiftyish-looking woman next to me with dyed black hair and a green dress looks at me and turns back to the window, as if she can make me disappear by not seeing me.

We're getting near my neighborhood, and I almost pull the cord to get off early. Maybe I could just take off, shed this life like my too-tight clothes. If I had enough money to buy a plane ticket, cash on the table, I could fly to Switzerland and have it taken care of. It. Gone. Zippo, like it never happened. No one would ever know, and I wouldn't have to worry about getting bombed in a clinic or called a baby killer. I could get back on the other side of this whole thing, where everybody else is, tsk-tsking at news reports about pregnant women putting their unborn babies at risk (translation: druggies, drinkers, not to mention compulsive joggers, roller-bladers, hot-tubbers, chronic antihistamine users). If Ted found out, he would probably forgive me, but there would always be something there and not there between us, like when you turn off a car engine and the sound of what you couldn't hear before fills your ears.

But who says I would come back, in that scenario? I could live out my life in Geneva. I could leave the miniature rental house on Tenth Street in Skokie, Illinois, with its three green rugs that came with the place and a few photographs of my parents and me in fading Kodak colors.

But no, I don't pull the cord and take a different bus to a different town. I decide I'm sticking around, like Socrates, or other important people who could have escaped their fate. I like to think this is my statement to society, my Apology. That in twenty years this all will mean something.

I get home and it's almost eight, and Ted stands up from the kitchen table, looking worried. At first he doesn't notice my belly because he's busy showing me just how worried he is, pacing. In fact, I don't blame him because these days people don't show up sometimes and then you never find them, and usually it's women, young women, with no one to claim them, no parents or husbands to search for them; at least, those are the ones you hear about on the news, their pictures floating over the shoulder of the newscaster like sorrowful angels, too contrasty, so that their eye shadow and lipstick look like bruises.

"I'm sorry I didn't call," I say.

My voice seems to snap him into really seeing me, not just the image of me he carries around with him all the time, like a photo in his wallet. He stares at my belly for a moment, then at my sweatpants and no makeup. "How far?" he asks.

"How far?" I repeat, confused. I knew pregnancy makes you sick, sleepy, weepy, sensitive to smells. But I didn't know how slow it would make my brain.

Ted sits down carefully in one of the green stackable plastic garden chairs we have around our dining-room table. "How far along are you?"

"About four months, I think."

"You think."

I nod. I was expecting him to throw his arms around me, to be stupidly ecstatic. But he seems irritated.

"So you've known."

I nod and sit down across from him. I push a bowl of bananas and grapes away from me; the sweet fermented smell is too much. The grapes stare back at me with round, sad faces. *I like you,* I say telepathically to them, *but I can't handle you right now.*

Now Ted's trying to decide whether to be angry or not. I can see him thinking it through, tapping a pen against the fruit bowl. I'm pissed, I'm not pissed, he seems to be saying with each tap, trying to figure out which one fits.

"Why didn't you say anything?"

Suddenly I feel like when I was a kid and I tried to explain to my mother why I loved cartoons so much. "Because no one gets hurt?" she suggested. She was driving me to first grade in the car she would die in eleven years later. It had always been a shitty car. I shook my head at her. I was still so little I couldn't think and talk at the same time. "Because the hero gets away with everything?" she tried again. This was in fact appealing to me, but it was something else, too: the physics of the cartoon, the way Bugs Bunny could pull a lampshade out of thin air and when he was done with it, it would disappear, no longer needed but not really discarded, just flickering beyond our vision. And if Elmer got soaked, he just shook off the water— no baths or tangles or towels to hang up. The economy of elements and movement transported me. That was what it really was, but I said something like, "Because everything's so clean."

"Clean?" my mother asked.

"All the colors and the water just goes away, and there's no dirt," I explained. But my mother didn't get it. She shrugged it off. And that was so frustrating, all the things she couldn't understand and didn't think were important.

This is how I feel right now with Ted, whom I met at the dentist office, who has many cavities, who apparently didn't

notice I haven't had a period in three months, who is trying to
stuff himself into the idea of fatherhood, like it's a jacket with
one arm. I feel for him, I really do.

"Nova, please talk to me," Ted says, and I can tell from the
tone of his voice that he's elected the not-pissed option and is
now trying to make sense of this, the way he does with city
planning projects, everything imposed on budgets and grids.

"I guess I wanted some privacy," I say, and that's the truth.
I dread the required monthly visits, the vials of my blood and
urine lining the stainless-steel counter, the parting and the
speculum sliding coolly in, my gynecologist Mary's round face
bending down to look closely, her breath against my thighs. I
squirm in my seat. A seam complains in my shirt.

Ted is looking at me like a man not quite recovered from
Novocain, mouth breathing and he doesn't even know it.

"Look," I say. "People tell you all kinds of shit when they
find out you're pregnant. They stick their hands on your
belly, and yesterday on the bus some woman was telling some
other pregnant woman about how when she went into labor,
she had to push on her hands and knees for ten hours. I can't
stand it!" I cry, and I rush from the table to our little bathroom and dry-heave over the toilet because I'm so hungry I
feel sick.

"Nova, honey, what can I do?" Ted says from the doorway.

"Orange juice," I gurgle, wiping my mouth with toilet
paper and heaving some more.

"OK," Ted says, running to the kitchen.

I lurch into the bedroom and crawl onto the bed and cry,
and once I get started it feels pretty good, and because the fact
is I'm not in love with Ted anymore, which isn't his fault, and
the idea of raising a child with him in this house with its low
ceilings and tiny doorways is too much for me to handle. It's a

house built for dwarfs. I don't think I can be Socrates. *You're not going to die,* I tell myself, but it doesn't help.

Ted sits down next to me and puts the juice on the nightstand. I drink it, and he strokes my back and says, "OK" to me over and over until I fall asleep. Later, he wakes me up and feeds me chicken and rice, and he tries to talk to me—I hear his voice deep in my ears as if underwater—but I'm too tired to do anything except chew and swallow with my eyes closed.

Friday morning there's not a pair of shoes I want to put on. It's too cold for flip-flops, but I finally decide on them even though it'll make the dentist frown. Maybe because it will make him frown. Ted offers to take me to work, but I decide to take the bus. If I'm going to be Socrates, I'm going all the way. I can feel my belly with every step to the bus shelter, bearing down on my lower back, telling me to forget those hipster stretch jeans, those platform sneakers, those years of relative freedom and anonymity. I pass women on the street and don't look at them, but I can feel them looking at me. I can spot a pregnant woman two blocks away, whether she's showing or not, her skin luminous with hormones, her eyes not quite focused. Older women, women maybe my mother's age, if she were still alive, stare hard at me because they know what's at the other end of this. They know, and they're deciding whether I can take it. I wish they'd tell me. I feel everything moving around me, a pressure on the skin. Men drive by wearing dark suits, looking straight ahead, purposeful. Sometimes a car slows down and a woman gets in.

On the bus, I sling my fare at Mario, who looks hurt. "Don't blame me, honey, I didn't get you knocked up," he says.

"But you wanted to, didn't you?" I say, watching his eyebrows fold down to his lids in a frown. I make my way down the aisle and imagine Mario pressing me naked onto a gray vinyl seat, pulling my ankles around his thick neck, drilling me, and here's the kicker: It turns me on.

I find an empty seat and stare out the streaked window, my belly jiggling as we roll over potholes and rumble, idling, at stop lights. I think of the bus as a giant metal womb, carrying us all to our entry into the world. This thought makes me look around and love everybody momentarily. But not for long. I feel a movement in my belly and can't decide if it's the bus or gas. I almost fall asleep and then, after a stop, the woman of the hands-and-knees labor plops down next to me. "So, when are you due?" she asks me, fixing smiling brown watery eyes on me, and I look around for another pregnant woman to direct her to. But there is no one.

"I don't know," I say. I can see her screaming, pushing, but somehow smiling through her labor, the happiest she's ever been.

"You don't know? Well, I'm sure you do know that if you're not getting proper care your child could be in danger."

"I don't want to talk about it," I say loudly, so that several people turn to look at us, and I turn away, but I can see her frown in the dusty window reflection anyway.

"You don't want to be a lousy mother, do you?" she hisses in my ear. Spit rattling in her teeth.

"I have an appointment, so piss off," I lie. I stare at her until she gets up and moves, glancing over at me every few minutes as if I might attack her. It isn't out of the question. I could've humored her for three more stops, I think. But I'm not going to humor anyone, I say to myself. I'm pregnant. They can humor me. I wish I could levitate like Jesus or Yoda out of this situation, float right above people's heads on a cloud of my wonderful-but-not-yet-clear-to-me destiny.

At the office, the dentist looks glum. "Low counts at the seminar," he grumbles to me as I hand him the day's files.

"Listen," I say. "Some people work."

The dentist frowns at my flip-flops. He has a ring of fat around his neck, and it seems to make it hard for him to breathe when he's upset.

"Well, I hope you know better, after all you've seen here," he says.

"Oh, believe me, I know better." This isn't exactly the truth, but it feels good to say it.

When I get home, I decide to call Mary the gynecologist, but I realize before I get to my front door that the offices are closed by now. It's sunset, and the trees around the cemetery across the street are flaring gold and red. A mother rabbit and several babies play around a particularly large, weathered gravestone. "It'll be both of us over there someday," I say to my belly, patting myself. This is the first thing I've said to my baby, and it occurs to me I could've tried to think of something more cheerful to say. But I don't.

I check the mailbox and look at Ted through the cut-glass front-door windows. He's pouring two glasses of red wine, and there are two brand-new candles lit on the table. Through the window, his edges fracture and blur.

He looks up when I come in, smiles. It's an I'm-gonna-be-a-father smile, all broad and silly. He's decided everything is definitely OK.

"I've made steak," he says to me, which is what he eats to celebrate. But I can't bear the thought of the glistening meat.

I drop my purse on the beige leatherette couch Ted's parents gave us. "Have you ever been to Switzerland?"

"What?" he asks. He brings me a glass, clinks his against mine. I hear a fizz and then I look down and realize he's bought sparkling grape juice. "I won't drink now that you can't," he says. He lifts his glass in a toast, his gray eyes serious and respectful, and I'm on the verge of telling him everything: the escape fantasies I've had, the other life we could lead.

But something makes me stop—maybe the way his face looks as fresh as when he stepped out of the shower this morning, not even a hint of beard shadow, the way his shirt is still tucked in so evenly, folded in pleats at the sides. I bring the glass to my lips, I drink in the sugar and the carbonation, and I imagine it flowing into my baby's belly, the bubbles sparkling in my womb like stars over an ocean.

"That's so refreshing," I say, and it's the truest thing I can think of at that moment.

After dinner, Ted takes the candles into the bedroom. "Leave the dishes," he says because that's my job, since he cooks.

"I don't think I can make love," I say down the hallway, where I hear Ted snapping the sheets back, setting the stage. He's ready to do it with a mother. He didn't know it when his sperm hit the mark, so this time is for confirmation.

"It's OK," he says, after a pause. "We can cuddle."

"I'm afraid I'll get sick if I lie down," I say, and this works. Ted comes back out of the glowing bedroom and sits next to me on the couch, where we watch a *Seinfeld* rerun on cable. Then I say, "It's a good thing we want this baby."

Ted nods and pulls me closer but doesn't say anything. George is chained to a hotel bed wearing boxer shorts and black socks, getting humiliated by a call girl. "Can I see you again?" he's asking as she walks out the door.

"Because, what if we didn't?" I ask. "Want it, I mean."

"But we do, don't we?" Ted says, with a look that says we definitely want it. I've got his attention now.

"But what if I didn't? You'd help me, wouldn't you?"

Ted clicks the mute, turns to face me, and the leatherette cushion squeaks under his stiff khakis. "Nova, what are you talking about?"

"I'm talking about Switzerland. I'm talking about—"

"Do you think I'm ignorant? Why don't you just say it?" Ted presses his fingertips to his forehead.

"So you wouldn't help me."

Ted doesn't say anything, so I don't either. I'm prepared to wait him out. Everything is very, very quiet.

Then he says, "Maybe we should get married?"

Now it's my turn to stare at the silent TV, Kramer frantically throwing open Jerry's door. The phone rings; it's next to my left elbow, but I don't move. Ted's looking at me, but I'm sitting very still, and then I definitely feel it, a wave in my belly, like floating in water except from the inside: the baby turning, signaling me.

Ted reaches across me and picks up the phone on the third ring. It's his mother in Florida. I can tell from how he says the "Oh, hi!"—his voice slightly higher, boyish in his throat. "Good news!"

I claw at his arm. I'm not ready for full disclosure. "Don't tell her yet," I whisper.

"What? Hang on a second, Mom." Ted puts the phone to his chest, and I imagine his heartbeat pulsing across the phone line, underground, under the Gulf to Siesta Key, where his mother sits in a white wicker porch chair with seashell-shaped cushions, and I can imagine her own heartbeat quickening, because when grown children reach a certain age, good news means babies.

"If you tell her, I am out of here," I say. I watch Ted's mouth get that Novocain look again, his eyes blinking fast as he puts the phone back to his ear.

"Oh, I'm back. Uh, the good news is Nova got a promotion . . . What? . . . Well, yeah, I know she's a receptionist. I guess it's more like a raise."

I can see Ted's mother with her sandy-blond breeze-ruffled hair, frowning slightly. I know she thinks Ted's too good for me because I barely took a stab at college and I'm thirty and working for an hourly wage. I know she thinks he could do better, and this makes me smile.

Ted reaches across me to hang up the phone and stands up. "I don't know about you, but I think this is good news. I think it's *great* news. I'm proud. I want to tell my family."

He looks so clean, so heroic. He could be a soldier with that determined jaw. "*This* is your family," I say, and I watch this wash over him. "Call her tomorrow," I say then. "I just wanted us to enjoy this on our own for tonight."

The muscles in his face relax, and he insists on picking me up and carrying me to the bedroom, lying me down on the cool, wrinkled sheets. He strokes my belly. "Are you sure you don't want to make love?"

No, I want to fuck, I think. *I want all holes filled at once.* I want to get worn out. My face heats, and I shake my head no. I pull him down next to me and curve my body around his, and as we fall asleep, I feel the fluttering in my belly again, pressed against his back, his good strong back, and I wonder what I will do without him.

I get up early Saturday, and I can't tell if the light in the eastern sky is sunrise or Chicago. I pick out the two or three things I can still wear and stuff them into a duffel the size of a body bag. I grab the yellow-green photos of my parents holding a small me, the lonely bottle of sparkling wine from the back of the fridge, and one candlestick and candle, just in case I feel like praying.

It's too early for the buses to be running, so I take Ted's car into town. On my way, I stop at a Flying J store ATM to empty my account, and then, on a lark, I decide to buy a bunch of beer. The clerk just stares at me as I pack like a hundred cans of beer into the duffel. I buy a couple dozen bottles of spring water, too. "Can you get this to my car for me?" I say, sticking out my belly. The clerk takes the bag, but he's scared of me. Maybe a little disgusted, too. He thinks he knows all about me—I've made the "bad mommy" category. But all he really knows is that I'm determined. He makes me walk out the door ahead of him.

I leave Ted's car at the Amtrak station just as the sky shifts from gray to pink. I consider going straight to the airport, but flying doesn't give a sense of the land, and I need to find a place where I can settle. I make the bellman carry my bag onboard.

"What you got in there, a body?" he jokes with me.

"Contraband," I say, with a big, friendly smile. We both laugh.

I never drink the beer, but I keep it near me, all the way to the West Coast, and I make bellmen move it for me even if I just change rows in coach. Nobody pays much attention to me on the train, maybe because I keep my hair combed and I'm behaving myself, reading and occasionally sipping a spring water. I like having a heavy bag; it gives me something to remember, something to take care of.

I try to think of a symbolic act for when I get out west, to celebrate my new life, like slinging the bag off a cliff, but that's littering and it wouldn't mean that I've really gotten rid of the past anyway. By the time I get to San Francisco, I can only fit in one of my pairs of sweats. My hips are sore from the narrow train bed. I'm too tired to go any farther, so I decide to stop, and this feels right, the way normal people make decisions. I check into a Motel 6 near the station and lie down on the wide bed, and I can see the small lump of my belly between my breasts. I take my parents' pictures out of their frames and spread them on my stomach and begin to introduce everyone.

Bulletproof Girl

That morning, Emery got a letter from her mother that
wasn't really a letter. Mail from her mother arrived often—
usually notes paper-clipped to neatly snipped articles, snap-
shots of her latest garden blooms or recipes for Tangy Thai
Salad and the like. Even now, when a heartfelt letter about
marriage and life's flux might have been appropriate, there was
nothing unusual about the crackle within the envelope, so she
didn't open it right away.

It had taken her an hour to work up the resolve to retrieve
her mail, delivered to the bank of brick-encased metal boxes
below her window as she'd drunk her coffee, her eyes burning
and puffy. The day before, she'd broken up with Liam, her
coworker at the PR agency in Richmond, where she'd spent
many hours building media lists while thinking up invite lists
for the wedding she felt sure would materialize. It was the
wedding she was grieving for, which, she knew, was rather sad.
How had she come to believe that a marriage was something
she should now acquire, like a car or a home mortgage? She'd
stayed up late the night before, watching *Diff'rent Strokes*
reruns and crying, worrying for her sanity, thinking about how
all the kid actors ended up robbing convenience stores and
OD'ing, and how this seemed somehow connected to her

own life. She'd watched *Cheers* and wished she could sit at that heavy bar and get chatted up by Sam Malone, drinking and drinking for free. She'd fallen asleep listening to an old James Taylor album on her turntable, saved from a garage sale, the vinyl sigh the sound of being outside in summertime with nothing to do.

Assisting this funk was her father's recent antics: complaining of aesthetic exhaustion, he'd moved into an apartment in a seafoam-and-white Victorian house around the corner from the lilac Victorian where she had grown up and where her mother still lived. Since then, she'd taken many calls from her mother, calls made from the house's empty third-floor ballroom with its triple-hung windows—Emery could hear the echo—during which her mother would retell the last conversation she'd had with Emery's father. He'd been gone nearly two months. The conversations were the same: Her mother would call to ask about an insurance policy—code talk for the state of their marriage, their future—and he would say simply, "I don't know." Or, worse: "You decide."

After sifting through bills and junk mail, Emery opened the envelope from her mother. It contained two items. One, a page torn from her mother's Vassar yearbook, senior year. There was her mother, third row down, almost indistinguishable from the other young women, their faces spare and big-eyed, their hair straight and parted in the middle. Everyone seemed to be brunette—even the blondes looked dark, a trick of the shadowy photography, which emphasized their smooth skin, the pale sweep of collarbones against tasteful necklines. Under her mother's photograph the inscription read: *May Bartlett, Senior, Miscellany News, 1,2,3,4; Night Owls 1,2,3,4; Vassarian, 3,4.*

Some of the women had signed their photos in round, certain script. One had written next to her picture, "Ready for your MRS? Ha!"

This, Emery thought, was unusual, her mother dissecting a yearbook. Looking for an explanatory note, she tipped the open envelope, and something slick twirled to the floor like a leaf. She bent to pick it up: a small contact print of three black-and-white shots of a naked woman standing with arms stiff at her sides, shot from the front, back, and side. The print showed the outline of the square, medium-format negatives, the numbered frames.

Emery looked at it in the light from the window. Then she dropped it as if it had begun to melt in her fingers.

This, too, was her mother.

She grabbed the envelope on the table, stared at the handwriting—definitely her mother's. She'd spoken to her only three days ago. Her mother had called to ask how she was, and Emery had actually been feeling quite terrible after an apartment-hunting argument with Liam, which had signaled the end of things, but she hadn't wanted to discuss it and risk touching off another listing from her mother of all the ways she had tried to please her father and all the corresponding ways in which she had failed.

She hunted for the phone, finding it in her bedsheets; she had fallen asleep with it in her hand. It had seemed important to know, at four in the morning, whether Liam had the confirmation number to cancel their reservations for a cruise. She knew this was exactly what her mother was doing with her father, calling about bills, and she shuddered as she dialed her mother's number. Busy signal. She turned on her TV for company and hit redial three more times with the same result.

On the TV, Oprah was announcing the show's theme: Surrender, with a capital "S." Emery dialed again and finally got a ring. She closed her eyes, listening for the universe (as another show's guest had advised), which at that moment sounded like the answering-machine message of her mother's voice reciting all nine digits of her home telephone number and instructions to leave a brief message along with the time of the call.

"Mom, pick up," Emery said. "Mom."

There was a brief clatter and then the squeal of the tape recorder. "Emery?"

"Hello? Hello, Mom. Cut off the machine."

"I'm trying! Hold on."

More clattering and then her mother came back on the line. "Hello, sweetie."

"Mind telling me what's going on?" Emery said. She felt exhausted all of a sudden, her voice cracking.

"You got my letter."

"Yes, as a matter of fact, I did—if you want to call it that."

There was rustling on the other end, a hollow thump.

"Hello?" Emery said.

"Sorry, I dropped the phone. I'm trying to get dressed here."

"Where are you going?" Emery asked. There was a new energy in her mother's voice that sounded almost manic. Emery had been home twice since her father had moved out. The first time, her mother had been crying too much to put on makeup or even make coffee; the tears spilling as if she'd caught a handful of dust in her eyes. On that first visit, the house still echoed with her father's leaving, which he'd planned in advance: furnished apartment selected, bag packed. He took so little and yet the rooms yawned with emptiness; Emery had felt it, too. She'd stayed the first week-end and had done everything her father usually did around the house, such as retrieve the morning paper, since her mother had been unable to acknowledge his absence with that simple act. And every weekend since then, she'd felt as if she should go home to at least distract her mother, who, it had seemed, was teetering on the edge of something; the yearbook page and negative she counted as further evidence of this. But now, her mother's voice was clipped and businesslike on the phone, the voice she'd heard nail down seating arrangements for a three-hundred-person charity event in a matter of hours. It didn't make sense.

"I'm going to see my attorney." Her mother paused, clearly to make Emery ask for more detail, but she was trying to catch her breath. She thought this meant divorce.

"You're not—you're not—"

"No, honey, I'm not divorcing your nutty father," her mother said. "Not yet, at least. I have decided to file a class-action suit against my alma mater. I've been on the phone all morning, calling classmates. It's been quite fun, really, catching up and all that. I've found an attorney who's willing to take the case on contingency, and so here we are."

Her mother had gone to Vassar at her own mother's insistence, the degree being a backup plan in case a Yale man didn't present himself. Instead, Emery's father had proposed to May over coffee while she was home for the summer on Long Island. He was a Ph.D. candidate from Ohio University, working construction during the break. Celeste, hopeful for an Ivy League alliance, hadn't taken it well. Emery was the peacemaker; born in 1967 when her mother was twenty-three and in her first year out of college. Her father landed a tenure-track job in history, and they stayed in Greensboro, a growing small town with parks and movie theatres, a good place for a young family. Her parents bought the old Victorian and rented rooms out when Emery was little to pay for the renovations. Everything had gone along very well for a long time.

"What are you suing for?" Emery asked. She picked up the yearbook page again, the paper waxy against her fingers, and then the print. There was her mother's young body, her gently sloped shoulders, small, upturned breasts, the dark pubis, and tiny crescents of fat just above and to the inside of each knee. There were faint tan lines from a one-piece swimsuit, her belly pale and tender looking. From behind, the shadow of spine, the twin dimples at the small of the back. Emery wanted to lie down: Those were her knees, her breasts, her dimples.

"I'm suing for the negative of the print I sent you," her mother said. "Institutionalized invasion of privacy, plain and simple."

Emery shook her head. "What are you talking about?" she demanded.

"Ever heard of W. H. Sheldon? Eugenics?" May paused again, and Emery waited for her to continue. "They were called posture pictures. A lot of schools did them, of men and women, particularly in the East, but some out west, too. Some contributed them to Sheldon's huge research project. Thousands of young men and women, sometimes with metal pins taped to their spines for his measurements—endomorphs, meso-morphs—is this ringing a bell?"

"No, it isn't," Emery said, dropping the contact print on the breakfast bar and rummaging through the kitchen junk drawer, hunting cigarettes. She usually stashed a pack behind the phone book for emergencies. *For medicinal purposes,* Celeste often said before a nip of bourbon. This appeared to be shap-ing into one.

"I'm surprised. There's been a small media frenzy about it recently. Anyway, Sheldon had already published his *Atlas of*

Men. Imagine, page after page of naked men. He was working on one for women. Your mother could have been famous."

Her mother was trying to make a joke. Emery didn't laugh. She felt her heartbeat speeding up, maybe from the coffee but also from a twinge of recognition. Her mother had done this before—calling in the middle of the night one year on her birthday, when Emery was a freshman in college, to tell her she felt like a failure, or, another time, burning in the backyard a box of girlhood journals Emery had never known existed, explaining she didn't want anyone to read them after she was gone. And there was that middle-of-the-night walk they'd taken once. Emery wasn't even sure it had really happened; possibly it had been a dream, like the time she'd floated out of her crib to touch the ceiling cracks. They'd never spoken of it, and though she often thought of asking, she didn't want to invite her mother into that territory, where she might do something else that Emery wouldn't be able to predict or understand. *Coming unhinged,* her mother had called it.

"So why send this to me, the way you did it?" Emery said, lighting up. "You're trying to scare some sense into me, warn me not to pose nude? I mean, I think we went over that, and God knows I'm happy to have taken the advice, with the Internet and all."

"They don't just hand these back to you, you know, when you graduate," her mother replied. Emery could hear the click of heels, car keys jingling. "I had to hunt mine down. Most of them were destroyed."

"Well, how did you get your hands on it, then?" Emery asked, taking a long drag. It was a menthol, a pack her friend Carla had left around, probably. She tried not to cough.

"That's a fair question," her mother said, all business now.

"But I have to run. I could call you later, or why don't you come down this weekend? I can lay it all out for you."

Emery exhaled. Sitting at home wondering if Liam would call had not been appealing, but coming home would not exactly be an escape. "I don't know."

"Are you smoking?" her mother asked. "Tell me you're not destroying those lovely pink lungs I gave you."

"No, no. I'm just taking a deep breath. I had a rough night."

"What happened?" her mother asked. "Damn, I'm late. Please come home. I miss you."

"OK, OK," Emery said. They hung up, and she looked at her mother's face in the contact print. Her lips formed a pained, straight line. It was the expression that came right before tears. Emery knew it well.

On the TV, Oprah was saying, "If you're in the water and you panic, you sink. The more you feel yourself sinking, the more you panic and thrash and begin to drown. When you stop thrashing, you can start to swim. Today we're going to talk about how to do it." Her glossy smile was wide and loving as she looked into the camera. Emery wanted to feel cradled by that gaze, but she couldn't concentrate. She stubbed out her cigarette and threw off her robe to get into the shower. Just then, the phone rang, and she plucked it from the couch where she'd tossed it. "Hello?" she breathed into the receiver, wondering if it would be her mother calling back, telling her she'd calmed down, or her father, or perhaps even Liam of the razor-sharp sideburns, fitted shirts, and unwillingness to commit to anything more than a six-month lease, though it didn't seem likely.

"Darling, it's Ci-Ci," her grandmother said, her rich voice caramel and pearl. She had lived on Ocracoke Island in the

Outer Banks for years, selling the house in New York after her second husband died. Now, Celeste's Long Island accent never emerged unless she was irritated or tired.

"Oh, Ci-Ci," Emery said. She could hear the ocean in the background, air gathering and receding.

"I tried to call you at work and they said you were off. It's a perfect day," Celeste said. "When are you coming to visit?"

Emery turned down the TV volume. "Have you talked to Mom?" she asked, perching on the couch arm.

"Not in a couple of days. Why?"

"How did she seem the last time you talked to her?" Emery asked, shivering now.

"Crazed with grief, per usual. I'm talking with her every other day since Gil left. I try to give her advice, but she won't listen."

It still surprised and thrilled her to hear Celeste speak of her mother that way; as a child, it had made her feel tolerant and superior, picturing May as the awkward, round-faced girl in her school photos. But now, she could see only the naked, grimacing young woman in the contact print. She knew exactly what Celeste would say about the letter—or the non-letter, but a message, nonetheless—she would say that May was being melodramatic again, theatrical. *Your mother wants to believe she's starring in her own movie,* Celeste used to say. *She wants attention; she was a needy child, always coming home from school crying over some imagined insult.* One time, Celeste had told Emery that she wished she had been her daughter instead. *You and I, we're cut from the same cloth,* she'd told Emery once. *Your mother is weak, and she wants everyone around her to make up for it.* Emery had been twelve, spending the summer with Celeste and writing an elaborate fantasy in her diary about running away, changing her identity, and living in an antebellum man-

sion in Charleston, Celeste's favorite city. Celeste's appraisal
of her mother had bound them in secret alliance against May,
one that made Emery feel alternately powerful and guilty.

"I'm sure she's still keeping herself busy, running errands,
ministering to the poor or something," Celeste continued, a
yawn implicit in her tone. "Are you all right?" she asked then,
as if aware that Emery's questioning might add up to something.

Emery closed her eyes. "Liam and I broke up," she said.
She let her voice trail off, watching Oprah move among the
audience, taking questions from earnest, shiny-faced women.
She was surprised that she didn't really want to talk about it;
she had simply used it as an explanation. Her disappointment
at the end of other relationships had typically been eclipsed
only by her desire to analyze every detail of their demise with
Carla, or even with Celeste. This time it was different.

"So you wanted to talk with a pro," Celeste said dryly.
Sometimes Celeste's cool dismissals irritated Emery, as much
as she felt warmed by her inclusion in them. "Now, Emery,
I'm serious. You need to come. I want," she paused. "I want to
talk with you. I feel I might float away otherwise." She added,
"And we can go on and on about Liam if you want. Maybe all
is not lost."

"Ci-Ci, I'm getting a call on the other line," Emery lied. "It
might be her. Or Dad. I'll call you back." They hung up, and,
before she got in the shower, Emery felt it necessary to slide her
mother's photographs—eager student and unwilling model—
into the cover of the envelope.

When May got back from her meeting, she clipped three lilies
and six daffodils to place on the dining-room table. She added
greenery, keeping it in groups of threes, as she had learned in

her arranging class at the Summerfield Gardening Institute. She chose a straight-lined, cylindrical glass vase rather than a hand-blown crystal one with yellow swirls, which would have coordinated far better, because she knew Emery preferred simplicity—she had a streak of the proletariat in her that May could only source to Emery's father Gilbert—Gil, as everyone except May called him. She didn't like the name Gil because it made her think of a fish thrown to dock, drowning in air, the iridescence draining from that delicate, blood-rimmed flap— and she also liked calling him by a different name because as his wife she was different to him than anyone else. At least until seven weeks ago.

She sat down in front of the vase of flowers to polish silverware and thought of May, the month of her birth, which it was now, and for which she was named. The directness of it, the bruising offhanded practicality that was her mother's style. It would be her fifty-first birthday in a couple of weeks, and her mother could still make her squirm, and her husband had left her because he was tired of everything she loved—dinner parties, boat shows, the annual Tour of Gardens—but these were the reasons to live! Beauty and people you knew, had known for years, the women trying new hairstyles as the years went by to camouflage their gentle aging, the men pulling their pants ever farther up their waists; it was life in the sweet mundane, and it had comforted her, though now she had to think about facing it alone. Even the forks had each other in their velvet case, May thought as she dropped in another. And the spoons, spooning.

Gilbert had been a perfect partner for her—he was handy, educated, willing to be a provider, in love with her. He could calm her when she felt she was losing herself—it was a weight- less feeling, really, quite the opposite of how people typically described depression, which was what her doctor had diagnosed years ago. Instead of feeling heavy and exhausted, she vibrated with an energy she couldn't control; she felt that at any moment she might burst into tears or into song; it was a terrible, razor-thin indecisiveness: Any second she could go one way or the other, and in her worst moments, she became so paralyzed by not knowing that she could only sit at the kitchen table and tremble. Gilbert was sympathetic to these spells, while her mother had berated her. He was a principled but mostly reasonable man, and he'd infuriated her mother by everything he was not—rich, connected, comfortable in cuff links. And May had loved him, too. Everything had fit into place so neatly that she'd spent that first year of her marriage, the year she'd gotten pregnant, fighting off a growing panic. She often found herself hesitating to pick up a glass for fear of breaking it.

Finally, she'd decided to grant herself at least one transgression in her life. She remembered the moment she'd thought of it: They were living in a garage apartment in Columbus while Gilbert finished defending his dissertation, and she was sitting on the scratchy couch staring at the blue-painted window frames. She was nauseous, and the blue seemed to vibrate against the white walls—why had someone painted the frames blue? She was trying to put on her shoes to go to the grocery store, but the thought of it made her want to cry and wretch at the same time. And in that moment, it had come to her: Someday, if she needed to, she could break any rule she wanted. She could have an affair. She could even kill someone if the situation warranted it. Anything, as long as she lived a good life in every other way. Then perhaps she could get away with her one crime, plead insanity.

Now, with the trip to Maryland and her raid of the

Smithsonian archives, she had used that up, too. The posture pictures were in storage there because the dozens of colleges and universities that had sponsored their creation no longer wanted them; after their discovery, many schools destroyed them, but a few had donated them as historical record.

So that's what she was now, she thought, as she closed the silverware box and went to the kitchen to chop cucumbers for a salad. Her body, a piece of history. She thought Gilbert might appreciate the irony of that, but she had no intention of telling him what she'd done. It joined a string of things she could no longer share with him because he had withdrawn his permission. No more laughing over headlines botched in the local paper, no more jokes from the office, no more *honey, guess what.* She'd thought she'd feel victorious stealing her negative, but instead she felt emptied, with a surprising twinge of humiliation. It was such a small thing, really, and yet she'd spent her coupon for breaking the rules.

She felt only a little ashamed at the drama of mailing the print to Emery to lure her home, including the yearbook page to ensure Emery made the connection. This was a familiar pattern, she knew; when she needed Emery, she sent out a signal, and Emery was always there for her. One night May had awakened her from bed when she was maybe nine or ten. She had not slept well for days; the prescription she'd been taking at the time only wired her more. She'd taken Emery for a walk around the neighborhood. At the time, in her sleep-deprived state, it seemed a carefree, whimsical idea—what mother and daughter shouldn't enjoy some girl time at any hour? But of course, she was half-crazed with exhaustion and the medication. She remembered Emery's fingers warm in her palm, her pale nightgown pressed against her child's belly as she quick-stepped to keep up. For weeks afterward, once her spell gave out and she was getting up at night only to go to the bathroom, Emery would appear at the door, blinking in the yellow light, asking if she wanted to take a walk. And now, she could hear her daughter's practical blue car pulling up the brick-paved drive, the slow whirr of tires over the herringbone pattern the sound of arrival.

She met Emery at the side door and hugged her, fingertips on the ridge of spine in her daughter's narrow back, and she resisted cupping the back of her head in her palm as she had done with her as a baby. Lately, time was folding over itself like a scarf dropped slowly to the floor; she was now thinking of Emery's purple-faced yowl on her first morning in the hospital, May tugging at the shoulder snaps of her gown, happily frantic to feed her, Gilbert watching her with gentle fascination in a chair next to the bed, as if he had only just discovered who she was. May could hardly remember anything of that first year of Emery's life except for that moment, and she swallowed to ease the sudden thickness in her throat as she released Emery and stepped back, allowing her to pass into the house.

Emery leaned to sniff the dining-table flowers, the plain vase a gesture of self-control May knew she wouldn't register.

"Can I get you some iced tea?" May asked.

"Wine," Emery said in the front room, then turning. "If you have any open?"

"I might," May said, walking to the kitchen in the back of the house, which overlooked the best of her gardens. Another gesture of self-control not to say, *Isn't it early to be having a drink?* In any case, it was mid-afternoon, and if they were to go out to a late lunch, it would not be out of the ordinary to order a glass. And, after all, she'd sent Emery quite a shock, or at least that had been her intention; one might want a drink, considering.

She'd planned what she was going to say about it, of course. Sally, her college roommate, had sent her an article about the posture pictures. The letter arrived right after Gil left. The article had only a short note clipped to it: "Wonder if they still have ours?"

There had been no question at that point. May flew to Maryland. She'd called Celeste and Emery twice, so they wouldn't miss her. She'd spent two days in the churchlike silence of the archives, posing as a research assistant, sitting in a thinly padded leather chair that hurt her hips and wearing white cotton gloves that reminded her of formal dances. After the first couple of hours, the archivist didn't watch her too closely. Stealing herself back—in miniature, her form dark and hollowed in negative, a pained defiance in her young face— had been the most frightening thing she'd ever done. But it had felt pointless until she decided to do something about it. Nothing like a little litigation to give one direction in life, she thought, as she found a bottle of white in the back of the fridge—she'd never been much of a drinker but had certainly appreciated the Xanax prescription her doctor had written after Gil left, careful to take only the dosage each day; this was how she protected herself from the shame of needing medica- tion at all—it was simply following orders, something at which she'd always excelled. For a long time, she'd told no one that she took prescriptions for depression; it was long before such a thing was acceptable, even fashionable, her friends casually comparing their dosages of Prozac. In recent years, she'd been able to go long stretches without needing anything at all. She'd thought she was getting better, until Gil had so deliberately shown her how wrong she was.

She poured herself some wine, too. She found Emery on the sunporch, her favorite room in the house. Emery had kicked off her sandals and tucked one tomato-polished set of toes under her thigh. "Thank you," Emery said, accepting the flowered paper napkin May handed her with only the slightest hint of irritation before smiling up at her as if to erase it; ever since taking a conservationist class at Wake, she'd decided paper napkins and towels and even facial tissue were wasteful. May knew this, but she could not give someone a drink without a napkin; it would be like wearing pumps without hose— something she'd also seen Emery do.

"Be right back," May said. She went upstairs to the spare bedroom she used as an office to retrieve her papers. Gilbert had chosen to tell her of his plans in the living room—*the leaving room,* one Russian exchange-student housekeeper had pronounced it, which seemed so achingly appropriate now—the room where they had cocktail parties and occasional student visits, not the bedroom, not the kitchen or the breakfast area where they shared their pot of coffee every morning. She'd seen several of her husband's colleagues leave their wives for co-eds, sometimes after twenty years of marriage or more, and she had asked Gilbert to just tell her; if that were the reason, she deserved to know. He'd said no, there wasn't another woman: *There is only you, and your desire to control everything. You want everything to be designed, arranged. It's suffocating.*

Well, perhaps he was right. All through her life, she'd done exactly what was expected of her—if one didn't count her failure to breed with an Ivy Leaguer—but she had been an obedient child and a good student and then had cheerfully forgone a career to become a devoted wife and mother. If she'd been given a job description, it would have said, near the top, "Arrange Everything." Every dentist appointment, catered reception, vacation, school activity, everything. She wasn't sure if she deserved to be left after nearly thirty years of marriage or the attendant humiliation that had led her to plead off several recent engagements due to sickness, which, she told herself, was not entirely a lie. But she was damn sure she had done her job.

Yes, she felt untouchable now, an outcast. She had even started taking her walks late at night instead of in the morning so she wouldn't run into anyone. Walking late also allowed her to surprise herself by arriving quite regularly at the corner near where Gilbert had rented a studio—why had he moved away only to stay so close? Most nights the hexagonal attic window was light filled; light or dark, she got no comfort from it, thinking of her husband in there, keeping himself from her. Emery had told her the room was practically bare, how his razor and comb balanced on the narrow, chipped sink edge in the closetlike bathroom—what fifty-five-year-old man would choose this over a feather bed and a woman who had aged well and loved him?

Downstairs again, May settled into the wicker loveseat across from Emery with a thick manila folder. "So let me bring you up-to-date on the situation so far," she said, settling her reading glasses on her nose.

"Great," Emery said. She had already nearly finished her wine.

"Pace yourself, darling," May said, eyeing her glass. Emery rolled her eyes; May ignored this along with her daughter's decidedly sarcastic tone. "I met with Mr. Peelson after we talked this morning, and he feels we have quite a strong case against Vassar and that in fact this could ignite a national controversy and force universities to be more accountable for their policies, past and present."

"Did he use the word 'ignite'?" Emery asked.

"I'm sorry?" May looked over her glasses at her daughter.

"I'm curious. Does he sense a PR opportunity here? Maybe the morning-show circuit, CNN?"

"Stop it, Emery."

Emery tossed back the rest of her wine. "Why are you doing this?"

"I've already explained to you—"

Emery set her glass on the stand. "No, really. What's the point? You want to get yourself in the national news for posing nude with, like, a million other women? You want that to be your claim to fame?"

May pulled the negative out of an envelope. "Look at it."

"I already have."

"No. Take it. Hold it up to the light," May said, leaning forward to put it in her daughter's hand. Emery obliged, tilting it toward the windows. "They had us line up in the gymnasium," May said. "You had to fill out a form and then get undressed. We held our clothes in our arms and waited our turn. A coach stood there with her clipboard and told me to stand on the masking-tape line. She told me to push my shoulders back and keep my arms straight at my sides. Everyone did it, Emery," May said. "Some girls cried, but I didn't." She was trying to say that she had resisted in some way, as well as she knew how.

"OK," Emery said. May could tell from the way she looked at her lap that she was humoring her. But for now, that was enough. "How did you get a hold of this, anyway?"

"I liberated it from the Smithsonian archives," May said. She tilted her chin up and regarded her shocked daughter.

"You stole it." Emery looked at May.

"It was mine," May said slowly.

"You're bringing a lawsuit based on stolen evidence," Emery said.

May didn't say anything.

"Mom?" The negative was pinched between her daughter's fingertips, quivering.

"Mr. Peelson says—"

Emery stood up. "If you think you got screwed on this photograph, just wait until you get to court," she said. She dropped the negative on May's lap. "I'm going to go lie down for a while," she said.

May watched her daughter climbing the curved staircase. She could see the light from the front windows blonding streaks in her hair, the line of her cheek and one arm, the bottoms of her feet, bare and pink and private, where her body met the wood. *I am doing this for you,* she thought.

Was she pleased with herself? Emery wondered, lying in her old bedroom. *Was this some way of saying that she could still surprise, that perhaps she was even more of a force to be reckoned with alone than safely married?* And this made her think of Liam. Had he seen some tendency in her to need too much? He had broken up with her at lunch. A place where they always took clients—shiny black tables, a sleek, dark-wood bar, liquor bottles glowing in front of a lit mirror, waiters who could go on and on about the ingredients of a sauce. She pulled her cell phone from her jacket pocket to call her father at his office.

"Hello?" he said, with that familiar questioning upswing on the "o."

"Hey, Dad."

"Hi! Are you at work?"

"No," she sighed. "I decided to take a couple days off and come home for a long weekend." It was a relief to have a normal conversation. Just the simple give-and-take of a greeting.

"You want to have dinner? If that works with everything," his voice trailed off.

Ah, more code talk now; she recognized it. Her parents talked about household finances, her mother relived strange college rituals, her father said the word "everything," and she was required to understand what he meant.

"Yes," she said. "Yes, that will work."

Emery heard her mother climbing the stairs and moving around in her bedroom—it felt strange to think of it as just her mother's room; it wasn't really, yet—and she came down the hall and stood in the doorway.

"I thought I'd take a nap, too," May said.

"That's good," Emery said. "Actually, I decided I'd meet Dad for dinner in a little while." She didn't look at May as she said it; she felt she was betraying her, but she wanted to see him.

May sat on the bed. "Are you going to tell him I've gone crazy?"

"No."

"But that's what you think." She didn't seem upset, just matter-of-fact.

Emery pinched the bridge of her nose and smoothed her eyebrows with her thumb and index finger. "No, I just don't see why you have to do this."

May said, "OK," and nothing else. But she watched her walk out and drive away, Emery knew.

On the way to her father's apartment, Emery thought of her mother posing for the posture pictures. What had it been like, going goosebumpy before the cold flash of the camera? Would she have submitted to it? It had angered her, yes, envisioning her mother standing docilely with her clothes hugged to her stomach, another woman easily ordered around.

Thinking of this, she wondered why she hadn't stood up and slapped Liam in the restaurant, why she hadn't done a single thing to make him feel as uncomfortable as she felt pained and betrayed. A simple answer would be the need to retain one's self-respect. But wasn't that just another way of saying behave yourself? Do what you're told? A man could fight in a bar and shake hands with his rival afterward. It was something to laugh off. A woman had to be concerned with holding on to her dignity, even if it meant stripping naked in front of strangers. Whatever the rule was, you followed it. And perhaps, she thought now, this logic had been related to her decision to marry Liam. It was time, after all. She was nearly twenty-eight. And it would have been a gift, yes, to her mother, if not her father. To replace the broken marriage with a new one. To create a certain momentum that might repair past injury.

She climbed the oyster-colored front steps of the house where her father now lived and rang the buzzer under the box labeled Caspin. After a few seconds, she heard her father's heavy step on the stairs near the front door, sounding as he always had at home.

He opened the door and smiled to see her, and he looked no different to her—graying hair parted on one side, hazel eyes shadowed by unruly brows, long hands hooked into his trouser pockets, his height a thing that still seemed to surprise him, how he rounded his shoulders and dipped his head forward in a sheepish, friendly way. Emery hugged him, heard the low thud of his heartbeat. "So, where to?" she asked.

"The Exchange," he said, patting his back pocket and front for wallet and keys, then pulling the door closed behind him.

At dinner she ordered a salad, thinking that since it was still early, she should eat light so as not to preclude eating with her mother as well, and she thought this was how it had been for friends of hers who'd grown up with divorced parents—two of everything, all that extra time spent in keeping divisions where they belonged.

"So, how's the apartment?" she asked. She looked for any reaction on his part, a stiffening of the shoulders, but he was just chewing his pasta, relaxed as ever. He had not tried to make a case with her for his actions. They hadn't discussed it at all except for the facts of the situation—he had moved out; he had no plans beyond that. In fact, in the weeks since her father had left, Emery hadn't asked him for his reasons. She hadn't been able to get past a silent injunction: *Don't do this.* Her focus had been on comforting her mother, and her father didn't seem to resent this.

He looked regretful, as if he'd forgotten something important. "I'm never there," he said, shrugging, as if that had been all the answer she'd needed. In her experience, he had never been prone to sudden decisions. He was a man of careful routines, with a scholarly view of the present as merely a lens through which one viewed history retelling itself. He had been the tougher one in parenting, with her mother often negotiating between them. He'd believed in thinking things through. *Think,* he used to say to her when he disagreed with her actions. Now she wanted to say the same to him.

"So, what's going to happen next?" she asked. Liam had broken up with a similar question. *Where do you see this going?* And she'd known then. A question like that. Of course, she had sent it right back across the table to him, exactly what he'd wanted her to do. And he'd said he was fine with living together if she wanted, but he couldn't guarantee anything. *There are just too many variables right now,* he'd said. She could feel her lungs tightening in her chest—this was the speech you gave to clients when proposing a new ad campaign. It was how you prepared them for failure, just in case. She wondered if he even realized it, or cared.

"I don't know, Emery."

The sound of her father saying her name cowed her. She was hungry and tired, and she knew this was adding to a certain shakiness rising again in her chest. When Liam had finished his speech, she'd simply stood up, slid her purse over her arm, and walked out, and her first thought had been of Celeste, how proud she'd be at this show of toughness. A show had been all it was. Of course, she'd expected Liam to come after her, then to knock on her closed office door, then to call her at home. None of it had happened. She tried to keep an even tone. "Is there something you do know? Right now?"

Her father sighed. "When you're young, you think you can live with anything, but that's not necessarily true," he said. He paused, as if considering something more to say, then shook his head. "Now, let's talk about you. Tell me what's happening in your world."

Emery didn't particularly want to talk about her world, which included Liam dropping her as smoothly as he ordered sushi and her mother ranting over a lawsuit.

She squeezed the edges of her seat. "It must have been something, right?" she said. "I mean, she did something, or you did something." Emery was thinking of Liam. It had all centered on the apartment and how things looked as opposed to how they were. Only weeks before, Liam had asked her to move in with him, and she'd asked him if this meant he wanted to get married. He'd asked for time to think. Then, looking at apartments together, she'd asked him again, and he'd said to her, exasperated, "Isn't this enough? I mean, what in this picture won't look like we're married?" Meaning what is seen is what counts. That was enough for him.

Her father's eyes snapped to meet hers. The resigned expression was gone. "You know I've always been open with you," he said. "I've tried to be. But there's a line, honey."

Emery nodded, a gesture of letting go. But she knew there had been something to cause the failure—or the realization of it. And she knew what she feared: ending up with her own resentful, then absent, husband. Running off to dig up remnants of her past and scaring her children.

Now her father was talking about time. "After so many years," he said, "you can't add it up to any one thing." His threaded fingers a small fence between them.

Driving back to the lilac Victorian, she felt for the first time a dull wedge of anger toward her father, pushing from her stomach. Her father had asked her to look out for her mother when he'd hugged her good-bye. *That's your job,* she'd wanted to say. *Remember? The wedding, etcetera?* It was possible, she knew, that her resentment was tangled up with what she felt about Liam. In the first few weeks after her father had left, she'd been very accepting, actually. These things happened. You couldn't predict it. She'd come home to help her mother. She was a good daughter. But now she realized she'd been so cheerful because she'd believed it was a momentary eclipse of reason on his part. He would come home, and there would be tearful negotiation and calls for counseling and then a resettling into the old routines—her mother ordering her father around, and he shuffling along obediently. What would he do without such guidance? But she knew she was asking what she would do without it, her parents' lives no longer a story she recognized.

It was a little after eight, pale stars emerging in the blue-gray sky, cool air sliding in the open windows, just the sort of spring night that would draw Celeste out to her deck, smoking one of the three cigarettes she allowed herself a day and watching the dark whisper of the sound. Emery dialed her number, listened to the rings. Celeste had no answering machine, laughingly explaining that she was an old woman who never went out—who would call? She took walks in the early morning and in the evening anywhere between five and eight, depending on the season and the length of the light, so it was possible that she was on the beach.

Emery plugged her phone into the car charger while waiting for a light. She had the weekend until she had to face Liam again. They shared several clients. The thought of having to work with him made her feel lightheaded from nerves. It amazed her how only days before he'd been the focus of her future plans—or illusions, as it turned out—and now she dreaded having to see him. She didn't want to let Liam chase her out of her job, but she didn't want to allow him to see her every day, the woman he'd rejected.

The light changed, and she drove along more slowly than she needed to. The truth was, everything had gone along so easily for a while that she was out of practice with disappointment. Her life had kept its own rhythm—first with the comforting swell and break of semesters, then, even at the agency, another rhythm: busy first and second quarters, slow third quarters when everyone took vacations, and then the bustle of fourth quarter, the snap of fall air and the end of the year within sight. And in her personal life, a new boyfriend each year, usually in spring, ending in winter, just after the holiday parties, no questions about whether it was time to meet the parents. She had laughed with friends that her relationships grew like plants. And she did not have a green thumb.

But Liam had been different. First of all, she had begun dating him in the fall, and she'd known him professionally for two years. He'd seemed to be a grown-up; thirty-two, gallant with clients. He could laugh at what he did for a living. "It's all branding," he'd say. "You've got the campaign, the collateral, the packaging. The client always pays." Liam took care of his accounts, and he took care of himself. He didn't see anything wrong with using concealer when he had a blemish. Emery didn't see anything wrong with it for herself but she did for him. This was what made her old-fashioned. This and wanting answers from him to questions like, *What next?*

In the looks department, they'd had it made. They were snappy, hip, young, living in a small American city. They sparkled like a commercial, going to dinner, then to a club. Once, a woman asked Liam for his autograph, mistaking him for an actor. Emery had even seen her dream in a commercial: a woman, lightly made-up and wearing a flowered camisole, kneeling in a garden in front of a lemon-yellow, French-doored house, dropping seeds into loose, black dirt. The husband arrives with wheelbarrow. He leans over her, watching her and smiling; their child runs laughing across the frame. It was selling seeds! It was all about what happens next.

At the house, the front door stood open, which was unusual. Emery parked her car at the top of the drive and walked quietly in the side door, thinking briefly of intruders, disaster. She thought again of that night when she was nine and her mother had coaxed her from bed. Her hair had been longer then, pushed behind her ears, and in the dark room her features were soft, girlish. What had she said to her? *Walk with me, and we'll tell ourselves a story.* Something like that. But Emery didn't remember any story. She wondered if her mother were even home, or whether she might be up in the ballroom, talking on the phone, unaware. Emery rounded the corner into the kitchen and saw her mother through the doorway, sitting at the dining-room table, elbows propping her folded hands against her lips. "Hi, Mom," she said quietly.

May turned and Emery could see then that she had been crying; eye makeup had pooled in the hollows under her eyes, the delicate skin reddened and papery. "Mom, what is it?"

"You're right. I might in fact be going crazy," she said, taking Emery's arm, the sound of her crying like someone suffocating.

It was her second outburst in less than a week. If May were to be honest with herself, she had to count the yearbook page and negative mailing as an outburst. But she'd felt only a little guilty when her daughter insisted that she accompany her on a drive to the coast the next day, where they would take a two-hour ferry across the sound to Ocracoke. Emery drove May's Camry, and May stared at the bleached roadside, trying to prepare herself for seeing Celeste. *That woman,* May thought. She could not make a list long enough for all the ways Celeste had failed, undermined, and generally depressed her. *I'm a control freak?* she'd said to Gilbert the day he'd left. *I'm half-stoned with relaxation compared with this woman.* For example, to teach May about responsibility when May had lost her house key, Celeste had waited a week to replace it, and May wandered the streets on the afternoons she hadn't been able to go home with someone. She wasn't sure that the trip to the coast was really a good idea. But her daughter had suggested it, and that was enough, someone wanting her to come somewhere.

Sending the letter to Emery had been a third option, not the one May had had in mind the day she'd left the Smithsonian with the negative in the waistband of her underwear. At first she thought she would keep it. Frame it, even. Then she thought she might destroy it. But on that first night home, she had not been able to decide, and it was the indecision that had enraged her. She dragged box after box down from the attic until she found her *Vassarians*. She wanted to see the face of the girl who had stood so placidly before the camera in the Kenyon Hall gymnasium. She remembered the air on her skin, the way she felt every quiver of her flesh as she walked—her inner thighs, her upper arms, buttocks, and belly—she'd spent countless hours inspecting every detail of herself growing up and yet no amount of vicious self-scrutiny could compare with being led to the masking-tape line and told to stand with her shoulders back.

She didn't remember being angry, only humiliated. Wanting it to be over. At the time, many women speculated that their photos would find their way somehow to be sold at Yale frat parties, and this had sparked two sorts of fear in May—one, that such a thing might happen, and, two, that no one would want to buy her photo. And maybe because of those twin fears, she'd put it behind her and hadn't thought about it for years. Now, however, she wanted to burn down Kenyon Hall. She wanted to find the photographer and the other woman with the clipboard—a physical education teacher?—and strip them in the street. When she'd talked with her old roommate Sally about it, Sally had only laughed. "We were little order-followers back then, weren't we?" she'd said. "Anyway, it's ancient history." So May didn't tell her about her plans.

And, once she was home again, staring at herself in her yearbooks, she realized she wanted to show it to Emery. But not in person, Emery patiently inspecting it, the historical record. She didn't want to make it comfortable. She'd made a contact print in a university darkroom, surprised at how easily she'd remembered the process from the *Art of Photography* class she'd taken her senior year. She'd wrapped it in the yearbook page and sent it to show Emery that the women in those school pictures—groomed, privileged heads tilted in just the same intelligent, lovely way to indicate they could be professionals or professionals' wives, whatever was asked of them—were also weak-willed enough to stand in line with the muggy gymnasium air hardening their nipples, sucking in their bellies to be photographed like specimens. *What if they had told us we needed to bend over, too, spread ourselves—would we have done it?* May thought. She'd sent the print as a signal, to bring Emery home, true, because she could feel a panic spreading in her chest, the worst she'd felt in years. Anyone could tell her that this was perfectly normal, that having your spouse of nearly thirty years move out on you would shake even the stoutest temperament. But she'd also sent it as a warning. She believed she was connected to Emery in a way her daughter could never admit. She'd always known when she was in distress, even before Emery had known. Gilbert had written this off. *If you always worry, eventually you'll be right,* he'd said. But she'd known when Emery had a bad day at school. She'd known when Emery cried every day during her week at Girl Scout camp—she'd felt it and had considered driving there one day just to see if she wanted to leave. Gilbert had said no to this. *She has to learn to depend on herself,* he'd said. In fact, she knew there was something wrong with Emery even now, though her daughter was driving so confidently next to her, chin tilted up like that—certainly no one could ever talk her into something she didn't want to do. How had she made a woman like that?

"Did I tell you about when I was in the hospital with you,

and there were workmen adding on a wing, and the hammering sounded like boat riggings in a marina?" May asked.

Emery nodded. "I think so."

"It made me think of Ocracoke," May said. "Your grandmother had just moved down there." May thought then of her labor: a tightening, then a balling of muscle that had squeezed her breath and made her ears burn. She remembered a series of three chambers opening inside of her, each wider than the first. She could close her eyes now and still go there, the muscles straining into arches, how she learned to let each contraction wave over her, breathing deeply and evenly. It was like trying to convince herself to breathe underwater, but she did it.

And then the pushing. She remembered that the urge to push was like a shuddering, like something flying loose in a machine, and the only thing to do was to bear down. She heard the nurse on her left, counting through the pushes, but by then she had gone inside her screams, in the dome of her belly with her child, in that blood dark. When Emery was finally out, the doctor held her curled body, rubbed her with a warm cloth. As the doctor lifted Emery toward her, she saw the yellow sheen of the umbilical cord, felt Emery's warm weight between her breasts. She remembered saying, "I'm sorry," and she was apologizing for her panic, for being weak.

"Mom?" Emery was saying. She had been speaking, May realized now.

"Yes? Sorry. Daydreaming."

"I was just saying that Liam and I broke up."

May turned to her. "What happened, honey?" She stopped herself. "Are you OK?" The conscious decision for self-control right then, to not ask everything she wanted to ask, to wait.

She tucked a wisp of hair behind her daughter's ear just to have a reason to touch her.

"I'm OK," Emery said. "It was just the other night, before I came. So I'm not sure I've really realized it yet. But it'll be there, waiting for me, right?" She smiled, and May couldn't help herself; she nodded in agreement.

Of course, Celeste would argue that you could make the past disappear simply by denying it. She claimed she remembered almost nothing of her parents or of her own childhood; she knew only that they had come to America from Greece before she was born and that she was their only child after a boy who died. Celeste had said her mother never learned English, and her father owned a shoe store. Both had died young, and she'd spent the rest of her youth in a shelter for orphaned and runaway girls. Her first marriage was an escape, the second a partnership. May wondered how her mother could deny memory, cut the past away like a callous. She had always thought Celeste was simply more realistic; she saw everything in terms of its use. May saw things in terms of her need—for beauty, love, comfort. This was a crucial difference, May knew, the thing that had made her so apologetic to doctors, her mother, her husband. She was done with it.

Emery led the way to the front of Celeste's house. Behind them, the sound was flat as glass and turning purple. The boathouse shadowed Celeste's small outboard and canoe. She could see Celeste through the picture window coming to greet them, her red shift a low flame. The dock cut through cattails and ended at a brief sandy path, which led to the steps, which May and Emery climbed to meet Celeste on the wooden deck. Celeste hugged them both but kissed Emery, too. "Wine?" she offered.

May looked down to smooth her linen jacket, hesitating, and Emery saw Celeste's head twitch just slightly in irritation. She smiled, patted May's shoulder. "I'll just bring the glasses, and then you can decide."

Emery followed her into the galley kitchen and helped her pour. Through the back windows, she could see how the setting sun lit the dunes across the road, turning the grasses orange. "Oh, I love it here, Ci-Ci," Emery said, sighing and closing her eyes.

Celeste picked up two glasses, and Emery took the third and the bottle. "Good. Then you should stay," she said, nudging open the screen door with her foot, waiting for her to follow.

May sat in one of the Adirondacks; Emery sat next to her. "I've always preferred this view to the ocean side," May said. She accepted a glass from Celeste without comment.

Celeste remained standing, as if preparing for a speech. "I'd like for us to do something together tomorrow," she said then. She stopped, waiting to be prompted for more.

Emery glanced at her mother. She believed she could see the muscles tightening in May's neck, bracing. That was one thing May and Celeste had in common: their dislike for surprises. Celeste had told her once that she'd rehearsed the most important scenes of her life—practiced smiling and slowly shaking her head in disbelief as she'd accepted the marriage proposals of her first and second husbands, both of which she'd anticipated, having never been interested in men whose actions she couldn't predict. "I don't think it's fair to people to not be prepared for them," she had explained.

May shifted in her seat. "OK, then," she said.

"It's ridiculous not to think about the inevitable," Celeste said, pausing to sip her wine. "Tomorrow, I am going to buy an urn. I would also like to go over my burial plans with you both, and I've made copies of my will."

Emery didn't know what reaction Celeste was anticipating, but she felt fairly sure it didn't take the form of May pretending not to have heard, gazing at the sound. Emery remembered a conversation she'd had with Celeste years ago, while she was still in college. She had come down for spring break, and they had sat on the beach one morning eating Celeste's homemade biscuits and drinking fresh-squeezed orange juice. Celeste's doctor had found a precancerous cyst on one of her ovaries, and she was scheduled to have a full hysterectomy. Celeste had told her first, left it to her to relay the message to May. *Look at the water,* Celeste had said. *It isn't just one thing. Every wave has a face, a lip, a crest.* Emery knew she was leading up to something; she was willing to wait, the biscuit warm in her mouth, the bright-blue blanket they sat on like a square of water, rippling around them. She watched a wave folding over, the glassy blue chamber that formed for an instant, a trembling helical room. Then it closed, rolling into itself, rising again— breathing. *The day it stops being a pleasure to watch this is when I'll let go,* Celeste said then. At the time, Emery had tried to act nonchalant—this was the kind of thing two adults talked about, and she didn't want to make Celeste think she couldn't handle it. Even then, she knew Celeste had told her this secret, like so many others, to bind them.

May tapped her wineglass with the inside of the wedding ring she still wore. The shadow of the house was long across the deck. "Well, you're right. We should make a day of it—it'll be more fun than I've had in a while."

Celeste smiled tolerantly at May. "Of course, dear," she said. She half-turned to the doorway, then back again. "You know, if you let go of the idea that he'll come back, you won't be so unhappy," she said. She looked at Emery then, in a way that asked for her support, a returned smile, but Emery looked at her lap. She knew the remark had been meant for May, but it had stung her, too. She knew she was still hanging on to Liam, her body missing him, too, the way the hand curls after carrying something for hours. She knew she would do her best to pretend otherwise until the feelings passed. She also knew Celeste had realized this, judging from the way she bit her lip, a rare expression of regret. But she wasn't one for apologies. "I think I'll take my walk and go to bed," she said then, leaving them on the deck.

Emery fought the urge to get up and follow her. She wanted to know what the business about the urn meant—was Celeste even now choreographing her death scene? It would have pained Celeste to be compared with May, but right then, Emery could see a real connection. *A little drama with your wine, ladies?* she wanted to say, but she didn't.

She was tired from traveling; her body felt heavy with it, but even so, she asked her mother for a Xanax. They would share a bed in Celeste's house, and Emery hadn't shared a bed with anyone but Liam for two years. She didn't know how she'd sleep. Her mother pulled the bottle from the purse, shook half a pill into each of their palms. They laughed about it, washing their pills down with the last of their wine.

"We should be movie stars with such habits," May said.

Emery said, without thinking, "Perhaps I'll have some nude photos made, to be revealed later in life." It was not the best joke she'd made in a while.

"You know, those photographs were mandatory," May said. "Nobody questioned it."

"You could have," Emery said. She wanted to say that

sometimes you had to make tough decisions. Sometimes you had to say no to something you wanted, like acceptance, or comfort, because it was the right thing to do. *People will let you be weak,* Celeste had said many times before. *They want you to be weak.*

"My mother would have called me a coward for *not* going along with it," she said. "She probably would've reminded me of the group delousing showers her parents had to take on Ellis Island."

Emery rubbed her eyes. It was true; she thought her mother had gone a little crazy, cooking up this whole lawsuit to give her anger somewhere to go. And what if she were right? What would that fact change? "I'm sorry," she said.

May looked at the dark window. "You know, it is sad, really," she said then. "They took us in our best years and turned us into things. They look like morgue shots."

The next morning, they caught the ferry from Ocracoke to Hatteras. On the ferry deck, May got out of the car, and when Emery asked if Celeste wanted to get out, too, she shook her head. "Too much wind," she said. But Emery knew this wasn't entirely the reason. Other than sunburns and brightly colored shirts, this was one way the tourists could be discerned from the locals—the locals stayed in their cars, windows rolled down, tanned arms resting on the doors, but the tourists got out to turn their faces to the sun.

Emery followed May to the front of the ferry, where the wind was strongest. The water was glassy near the sound, choppy past the island point. Here and there, rocks glimmered under the breaking waves. Emery could see Celeste in it all— the color of her skin in the sand, her eyes in the water, her hair in the thin, passing clouds—and she could see the summers she'd spent barefoot, wearing the same cut-offs until they were bleached and salt stiff. Coming back when school started, she'd felt choked by the lack of wind, her toes squirming in shoes, cloth chafing her legs. She'd felt as trapped as her mother seemed to just then, staring at the water, jaw set.

"Do you think they sell urns in designer colors?" Emery asked, nudging her.

Her mother managed a tight smile. "We can only hope."

They drove into Hatteras, past surf shops and fish houses, to the old part of the village, where, in a small clapboard house with "Taylor Funeral Supplies" painted in red over the door, they found urns displayed on a shallow bookshelf labeled "Floor Samples." The wider ones protruded, threatening to topple at the slightest shoulder brush. Emery ran her fingers over a miniature coffinlike brass model, and another that looked like a humidor, and then a granite one that looked like a smooth-sided Eiffel Tower or a perfume bottle.

An old man wearing a faded blue dress shirt and sagging khakis emerged from a curtained back room and stood a few feet away from them, chewing at something between his front teeth, lips working. "They's pyramids, towers, obelisks, boxes, and your customs. You looking for a certain kind?" he asked, his accent thick, coastal.

May stood stiffly, staring out the salt-clouded window. Celeste, addressing the room in general, said, "I want something simple, whatever is standard."

The old man nodded. "I'd say this box then. Brass or wood." He picked the brass one up shakily and handed it to Celeste, who inspected it, then passed it to Emery. She took the cool weight and looked at her mother, but May gave no indication that she was even aware of the conversation.

"Do you like it?" Celeste asked them both.

"It's fine," Emery said. She wanted to laugh again at the oddness of it, shopping as if for a dress or a couch. Then May seemed to wake from her daydream. She turned to Celeste, squared her shoulders. "You're right—this really is ridiculous," she said. She turned to the old man, who seemed unfazed by her outburst. "Here," she reached in her purse and handed him some bills. "Will a hundred do?"

"It's not so dear, I dun think," he said.

"Keep it," May said and walked out, shell strings rattling on the slammed door.

Emery started to follow her, but Celeste touched her arm. "Let her stew," she said. "Let's have lunch." She smiled brightly.

Emery knew she was asking her to choose. The urn had warmed in her hands; she shifted its weight to her hip, like a thick book, holding it like a schoolgirl would, and that's how she felt right then, dragged along on a surreal field trip. The man stood a few feet away, counting the money. He raised his head. "Tha's a sample, now. I'll fetch a new one, in a box."

"You must be joking," Celeste said to him, hand on her hip—Emery had seen this before, how Celeste could freeze people with a glance. The man flinched, went back to counting. Celeste turned to her again. "Let's go now."

"I can't let her go off alone," Emery said.

"She's not a child," Celeste said, looking childlike herself just then, brushing silvery wisps of hair from her eyes.

"I can't, Ci-Ci," Emery said. She did rather wish for a box for the urn or at least a bag, preferably with handles. She wished for something that could carry them all out of there, jostle the memory out of them, so that they had to reintroduce themselves, start over. She pulled open the door. "Come on, let's catch up with her."

Celeste followed but shook her head. "I'll go see Nina at the Island Wares. Remember Nina?"

Celeste had taken Emery to Nina's house many times, with its boutique on the first floor, shell necklaces, muslin sundresses and straw hats, and, on the second floor, bead-strung doorways and incense burners next to silk floor pillows. She knew Celeste was asking if she remembered all those summers of her childhood, when she'd sat under the table and listened to the women talk, Celeste helping Nina string shells, the sherry they drank a fruit perfume that rose warm from their mouths when they kissed her. She said of course she did, she remembered. "Just come eat with us, Ci-Ci. Then you can have your sherry with Nina."

"You'll take care of that, won't you?" Celeste said, ignoring the invitation, fluttering her fingers at the urn.

The urn was heavy in Emery's arms; she wanted to sit down on the bright sidewalk. With the sun in her eyes, she felt lightheaded. She bowed her head, and the weight of it tilting forward reminded her of praying, something she hadn't done with any sincerity since childhood, and she thought then of how Celeste had once called praying a form of begging. But that was what she felt like doing. "Ci-Ci?" she asked. "Don't make me carry this. Please."

"You aren't going to collapse on me, too, are you?" Celeste said, head and hip cocked. But she touched Emery's forehead, as if to check her temperature. Emery knew Celeste's remark had been about her mother, and this time it irritated rather than thrilled her, though she tried not to show it.

"You were the one who asked me to come. You said you might float away," Emery said. "I don't want you to." She slid an arm around Celeste's waist.

Celeste looked down the street, as if considering, but

Emery felt the give in her back; she would come. "Fine then," she said, and Emery knew that her grandmother had to sound as if she were doing a favor by agreeing; she knew this the way she knew her way through her mother's darkened house—might as well call it what it had become—and the way she understood the code talk of her parents. Here she was, Emery thought, herding these women together, indignant as cats. Angry over things they couldn't control or get any comfort from. She did want to collapse, but it seemed necessary to explain to the tourists passing with their neon-zinced noses and wet towels yoking their necks how it came to be that she was walking down this sandy street with her grandmother on one arm and her grandmother's urn in the other. It seemed to be the kind of thing that could and should be clarified with a quick speech, so that the sunlight glinting off the metal box would catch fewer salt-reddened eyes, lead to fewer odd conclusions, though Emery could think of none odder, or sadder, than the truth: Celeste didn't like to urn shop alone, and May had ditched them in the showroom, and they had all been abandoned in one way or another.

Emery saw May sitting in her car where they'd parked down the street from the funeral-supplies store. May gripped the steering wheel as if the car were idling and she might at any moment decide to drive away.

"Mom?" Emery said, standing at the window.

"Is she conscious?" Celeste asked.

May didn't respond, except to turn the key in the ignition.

"You ride shotgun," Emery said to Celeste. "Come on."

Celeste looked down the street again, as if contemplating escape. Emery opened the car door and pushed the urn into her hands. "Here. You hold it for a while."

Celeste sat down but stashed the urn in the middle of the seat, between her and May. The two women looked straight ahead. Emery sighed and scooted to the middle of the backseat, where she could keep watch over them both.

May drove to the ferry parking lot just as the ferry chugged slowly to dock. No one spoke; May leaned her head against the seat and closed her eyes until it was time to board, and Celeste fiddled with the radio. But once their ferry had cut through the fat, slow waves of the sound, past the low rise of the island, once they'd rolled off the ramp and turned onto the road, May was all business, leaning forward at the wheel, the bumper a hair's width off the next car's. "Come on," she muttered. Three cars ahead of them were maintaining a stately twenty-five miles per hour; the speed limit was fifty-five. She edged into the oncoming lane. The three cars were still fairly close together, Emery noted, heels of her hands pressed into the backseat, but it was quite a distance to pass. "We're pretty near the house, Mom," she offered.

"For God's sake, May," Celeste said, gripping the door handle. "I only bought one urn."

"I bought it," May said, as she swung out to pass. Emery could now see a pickup coming in their direction, still a ways off down the straight line of road and probably in no hurry, but it was hard to tell with the heat shimmering off the pavement, so that it didn't seem to be advancing so much as expanding.

"Mom?" Emery said. It was clear within seconds that this would be a very tight pass. It crossed her mind that she should try to buckle herself in on one side or the other, but there wasn't time, and she couldn't look away.

The pickup started edging toward the opposite side of the road, the driver perhaps considering whether to roll onto the sandy shoulder. May stood on the gas; the Camry bucked and tugged into overdrive. The pickup's brights flashed; May was saying something about the bastards not letting her in. "Trying to kill us," she said, as she swerved back into their lane, inches off the front bumper of the procession's honking leader. Emery looked back at the pickup, which they had flashed past at a distance of less than thirty feet, it seemed. The driver, an older man, Emery had seen from the white glint of his hair, had pulled over.

"What in the hell has gotten into you?" Celeste yelled, looking back. "That was Milt Tucker, poor thing. I hope he didn't see me. Have you completely lost it?"

May swerved into Celeste's driveway, spraying sand and squealing to a stop. The gesturing driver behind them held down his horn, the sound waning like a siren as it passed. May dragged the parking brake up, cut the engine. "Oh, it's just like when you taught me to drive, clawing at your door handle when I was backing out of a parking space, like I was going to kill us at five miles per hour."

"I did not do that," Celeste said, flinging off her seatbelt so that the buckle hit the window.

"You were screaming."

"Stop it. You're crazy, gunning the engine, you always were."

Emery sat in the backseat, watching the two women flail their way out of the car like startled birds. "It was a parking space! A truck turned into our row and was sitting there waiting for me to pull out," May said. "With his turning signal on, I'll note, and you were raving that he was going to mow us down. You know, it's a wonder I'm still alive, when you think of it. How did I survive all these years without you dictating my every move?"

"You *have* lost your mind, haven't you!" Celeste yelled,

slamming her door shut as Emery got out. "How could you put us all in danger like that? What is wrong—"

May waved at Celeste's words as if shushing a child. She turned to Emery. "Let me tell you something I know. This society makes women beggars. You have to be beautiful and independent and weak and smart and innocent and great in bed. You have to be motherly and childlike and fuckable. And you—" She turned to point to Celeste. "You made it out as if it were my fault, all these years. I had trouble with that bargain? That was *my* problem? My husband has *left* me. How dare you ask me what's gotten into me. Or you—" She turned back to Emery. "Telling me I should have stood up for myself better." She stopped, shook her head, palmed her forehead.

"Don't cry," Emery heard herself saying, more of a plea than an attempt at comfort. Celeste stalked toward the house, blue dress billowing; she was muttering something, but Emery couldn't hear it.

"That's the main thing," May said. "Not to cry."

"That's not what I meant," Emery said, even though it had been; her mother had caught it exactly. Across the street, she could see how, above the dunes, a single electric line stitched a seam in the sky. She thought of Liam sitting across the slick tabletop from her, speaking in vagaries that added up to all the ways he didn't need her, and of her father at dinner with his threaded fingers holding back what he couldn't or wouldn't explain, and of her mother forcing her naked back into a straight line because that was what had been asked of her, that was the requirement in order for her to move into the rest of her life. She thought of that spring night when her mother led her downstairs into the quiet dark, how the cool air rose from the damp sidewalk—had it just been raining?—how it had circled her ankles and the hem of her nightgown, how she had stumbled, trying to keep up, to hear what her mother was say-ing. *Let's tell ourselves a story.* She remembered the sound of her mother's voice, her rushed words, her fingers brushing a mist from her mouth and cheeks. *I want to tell you about the day you were born, how, when they brought you to me and I fed you that first time, there were workmen outside the hospital, and their banging sounded like the wind-rattled riggings in the marina at Ocracoke, and the other newborns crying down the hall sounded like seagulls or cats begging fish,* she remembered that. *And I want to tell you that we are all born beggars, Emery. I realized it that day.* She believed her mother had been looking for comfort that night, yes, but that she had been trying to give it as well, long before the reasons to need it had presented themselves.

"I mean," Emery said, "tell me what I should do." She wanted to take her mother's hand again, be led along.

May bent to take the urn from the front seat. She straight-ened. "Do the thing that frightens you," she said, nodding to the light-veined water as if to convince herself. "I'll tell you something else that I think is true. If he doesn't come back, I can live with that." She was trying to smile, looking back at Emery now, but her expression reminded Emery of the girl in the negative, lips pressed together in that sad line, trying to make the best of a situation she couldn't control. That was what you did, Emery thought. You pushed your shoulders back and waited for the moment to be over, for when you could move again.

She followed her mother inside. May walked swiftly past Celeste and placed the urn on the mantel over the fireplace that Emery had never seen used—Celeste had arranged pots of dried geraniums and cattails on the hearth and circled them with a select collection of shells, conches larger than anyone had found on Ocracoke in years, curved driftwood smooth as skin.

Celeste watched May step back to observe the dull brass gleam of the urn. It sat between a desk clock and a photograph of Celeste with May and Gil and Emery from years ago, when Emery had been small enough to rest her cheek against Celeste's hip. Emery stared at her mother's back, then glanced at Celeste, trying to judge from her expression what she would do. *I'm the one who's scared,* she wanted to tell them both.

"It can be your shrine," May said without turning around, and to Emery's surprise, Celeste laughed, a quick exhalation.

"Better to have it now," she said.

Later, Emery set the table for dinner. She made a salad and cooked scallops in butter, lemon, and wine, while Celeste and May sat in the Adirondacks on the deck. Emery knew she'd have to leave soon, perhaps the next morning or certainly the day after that, catching the ferry near Styron's General Store on Silver Lake Harbor, crossing when the tide was pulling in, rescuing the crabs trapped in their warm pools. She knew she'd go back to work, but only long enough to look for another job. Maybe she'd move as well. Maybe she'd come home, just for a while, because she was needed. There had been times in her life, she'd admit it, usually when she found herself on a crowded street or in an airport or in a room full of people talking and laughing, when she'd feel as if she were frozen in glass or wrapped in steel. She'd look at people, how they'd sweat and bite their nails with wanting, and then she'd feel clean and hard. Bulletproof. But she thought now it might have been a lie she'd told herself, that she could ever cushion herself from need.

She could hear May and Celeste's voices threaded with the lift and sigh of the ocean. She lit the candles, poured glasses of white wine and cold water, and called them inside.

How to Clean Your Apartment

Clutter. *See also* **Choking, 4.33**
   boyfriends, 4.52
   mothers, 4.76

Let's think for a moment about why you're here. There is, first of all, the matter of the missing man, who convinced you to stay in this city of multiplexes and theme restaurants rather than run the "rat race" in more exciting locales. His arguments led you to expect certain outcomes. He came with a set of plans and operational instructions, which now, of course, are also missing.

And there is the matter of the pop-up mother, leaping across phone lines, from behind doorways, ever hopeful for your marriage and motherhood—words you hear echoed whenever she says, "I just want you to be happy." She means well, but with all this clutter you can't find your walls anymore, not even a window, and what you need more than anything is light.

There are women you know who would decide to climb Mount Kilimanjaro at a time like this. Or join the Peace Corps, or start a foundation for a new cause. You happen to believe haircuts are life-altering events. So you've decided to clean your apartment.

You have observed your life from many angles; you have wandered its rooms, cleared fire trails where you could. You have considered the years neatly appointed like the trimmed lawns on this charming college street, and the picture doesn't please you. *Bottom-line it,* as your boss says: The future is uncertain. It's time to take control, time to reclaim cubic feet of storage space in your closet, time to give the dog back his favorite corner, at least temporarily. How happy do you think he is, wedging himself between a pile of magazines and that dying plant? That will be your first step, you think with a tentative smile. Get rid of the plant—but save the clay pot; maybe you could fill it with marbles, use it as an umbrella holder, a doorstop.

Alcohol
as cleanser, 1.20

Yesterday afternoon, you stopped by the liquor store and brought home, in addition to a fifth of Jack Daniel's, several boxes. You bought whiskey because it's the stuff the lonely detective in your mind drinks, feet propped on a wooden desk, overcoat striped with slats of smoky light. It's the beverage of the tragic, the misunderstood. Night after night, you strain for sleep; your detective gave up on it long ago. He waits, he taps his desk, he's the one asking all those troublesome questions that rattle unanswered in your head. Clutter. What does your detective say? Get to the bottom of it. See what you find.

Use the liquor boxes to carry old clothes to Goodwill or to your friends, whoever's less picky. Warning: Offering your cast-offs to friends can be dangerous. You will find out what they really think of your personal style, or, worse, you might discover how much better they look in your clothes. There is no need for these revelations right now.

Start with the closet. The first items will be easy—you will pluck from its hanger the purple and chartreuse shirt with a stain on the breast pocket; you wore a funky brooch to cover it for a while, but then it lost its funk, and you lent it to a coworker and forgot about it when you decided to switch jobs, move south, *re*-reinvent yourself. The shirt doesn't fit your image anymore. It says cute; these days you're hip. Drop it in the Glenfiddich box. You're off to a very good start.

Wardrobe
role of Fate in women's, 3.43

There are good-luck clothes and bad-luck clothes, and you know that both must be handled with cautious respect. Good-luck clothes can lose their charm if you wear them too often. Bad-luck clothes can become good-luck clothes, given time, but you have to be willing to risk it, give them a second chance. Take, for example, the red dress you bought for that trip you took with the environmentalist, vegetarian, wine-collecting Silicon Valley programmer you met at a client's software launch party. You saw yourself wearing that dress while cruising Route 66 in his olive-green MG, a matching scarf tied around your neck and whipping with your hair in the wind. The day you wore it, the sun burned you both so thoroughly that you had to drive with the top up from then on; by day three, there was a constant ringing in your ears from the engine that roared like a lawn mower in your head. You were too hot to move—or cry—when the car finally overheated somewhere in the desert, at which point you discovered that Java and C++ certification is no guarantee of one's classic-convertible maintenance skills. Neither of you took it well; there was no further communication after the plane ride home, not even an e-mail.

You redeemed the dress in an interview (with the help of a rather boxy jacket, which now, too, must go), winning the job for which you later moved south. Still, you haven't worn it since, so drop it in the box.

Ah, here is the black velvet one the English yachtsman you dated in college bought for the Torquay Ball. You loved his accent and the fact that he could shinny up sixty-foot masts in horizontal rains while whistling and that he had sailed the North Atlantic alone. The night you wore that dress, the two of you danced for hours, until he compared you to the Gulf stream (hot and fast) and dipped you with unexpected clumsiness, pouring a very good champagne down your back. The dress is too, well, *fuzzy* for you now, and the last you heard, the sailor traded his boat for a bank. Walk the plank, you say, as it drops into the box.

Make that two boxes: In addition to the shirt, skirt, and dresses, you have ditched six pairs of shorts, a pair of pink leather pants you bought during a flu of bad taste, a jacket made of fabric curiously resembling couch upholstery, several T-shirts whose slogans don't fit your point of view anymore, nine lonely socks, several tattered belts, and many slips and nightgowns you never used. Actually, pat yourself on the back—no less than three teddies, two wizened garter belts, and seven slippery camisoles, the shrapnel of various past romances, have fallen gracefully into those boxes, as well. Be proud; you are moving on.

Screening calls
     brief arguments for, 7.61

The phone's ringing; you know who it is. He always calls at this time of day. All week you've let your voice mail field his messages, but this time, take a deep breath and answer. Remember what this day means to you; understand that nothing short of a complete break with all past encumbrances will leave you free to enjoy the future.

So.

Break the seal on that bottle of Jack Daniel's, and pour yourself a finger or two as you walk to the phone. Easy does it: Liquor will make you sentimental, and right now, in the long stretch of a Saturday afternoon, with blond streaks of light sliding over your cast-off belongings like a message from beyond, and this man calling you yet again, this man who is beginning to make you feel like a bass in a stocked pond—the only bass, as a matter of fact—that gets caught over and over again, held up to the camera by the professional fisherman and then tossed high over his shoulder, sparkles of light or water flash in your eyes, you can't tell which is which, you don't care. "That one looked a little worse for wear," the fisherman mutters, but no matter, he'll catch you again, you'll swim toward his newest array of cheap but shiny lures, wriggling with their shimmer, memory of past fish misjudgments triggered only when the hook rips in.

Answer on the fourth ring. Say hello in your deepest whiskey voice. Lean against the wall and listen as he tells you how sorry he is about last weekend; he wants to make it up to you, how about the two of you go to dinner, just to talk, he says.

Take a long sip. Let him do the asking, for a change, while

you review some facts. Don't be too hard on yourself. Remember that you did break up with him, at least, when he gave you the Space Speech—specifically, his needing more of it, your not giving him enough. He was going to be traveling more with work, he said; this was an uncertain time in his life. You nodded, tried to recall a time in your life that *hadn't* been uncertain as you closed the door behind him.

But then you broke down and called him last weekend and he came over, and you knew you could have, should have, asked questions before taking him to bed, but you also know yourself well, and you are most likely to trust someone when there's the least reason to do so.

After your less than prudent behavior, you secretly labeled him the man who is smarter than you. Your closest female friend says he's a fool—you yourself have told him he's a fool, but it doesn't make any difference. He must hold within him some secret, some divine strength, to be able to walk away from you so easily. He must be smarter than you to be able to stand being alone, while you circle the boat, drowning in the weight of your own memory.

But what better way to clear one's head than to get rid of all the things that hook one to the past? you think as he apologizes for last weekend. Let's go to dinner, he urges. Can I come pick you up? he asks. You want to say yes, you want him to come over, every part of you wants to raid that Glenfiddich box and cinch yourself into one of those garter belts you swore you'd never wear again, maybe slip that red dress over top, maybe not.

Close your eyes. Think about the beautiful, clever, independent woman you thought he saw when he met you. Be strong. Tell him you're in the middle of spring cleaning. Tell him you're streamlining your life.

Are you moving? he asks. Ignore the hint of regret you'd like to think you hear in his voice.

I hope so, you say.

Chrissie Hynde, condoms, junk mail usefulness of, 6.38

Put on some music to get the sound of his voice out of your head. You're in the mood for the Pretenders but Chrissie Hynde's voice makes your dog howl. Still, at this point, you need some of Chrissie's black-leather inspiration. Choose her second album, skip to the song called "Pack It Up." Ignore your dog, who is already cutting loose on the backup vocals, snout puckered at the ceiling. Look around your apartment for leftover evidence of the man who is smarter than you. All you find is a chewed toothbrush and a half-used pack of condoms—not the brand you usually buy. If you're having second thoughts about parting with these meager traces of his existence, remind yourself that the package was open when he first brought it over.

The toothbrush you'll toss, no problem. The condoms you'll keep; allow yourself to entertain the thought of using them with another man, the perfect man, the sweetest revenge. Except, you realize with a drop in your stomach that feels like a punch, the perfect man you're visualizing looks dead-on like the man who is smarter than you.

Concentrate on Chrissie. She knows how it is.

Dance while you gather the loose papers you find on your desk. Play air guitar as you shred the credit card offers, bank statements, career suggestions scribbled on airport cocktail napkins from your mother, expired coupons, guilty notes to yourself about long-term goals, crime reports and apartment-security ideas from your mother, mysterious phone numbers, invitations, and book suggestions from your mother, such as *Leading from the Heart* and *Ten Ways to Catapult Your Career*. Be encouraged that your discard pile is bigger, if only slightly, than your file pile.

Move on to the magazines, which you have shoved in corners, on top of shelves, behind furniture, under your bed. Don't get frustrated. Divide them according to title and year. Later you can go back and label the boxes, start your own magazine library: Beefeater and Cuervo Gold for the nineties, Absolut for the new century.

Therapy
cheaper alternatives to, 9.07

Give yourself a break before you take on the knickknacks. Add some ice to the Jack and have a seat on the stoop with your dog. It's evening, a dangerous time, as if the sun's not setting but losing its footing, slipping like your resolve. Ask yourself how you become such a hoarder of things. You weren't deprived as a child. Your parents had money, and they spent a lot of it on you, their only child, their straight-A student, their ballerina girl. They put you through lessons, braces, summer camps, private high school and college, new clothes every season, and even after your father had moved out, your slim-suited, banker mother came to every event in your young life. She came even when you didn't want her present. Like your first gynecological exam. Like the time in college you got booked for possession of marijuana and certain party-style mushrooms. After that episode, she had said it was a good thing you wanted to be a writer; it was the only profession left open to you.

That was just like her, you think, ever practical, impossible to ruffle. Your mother had more garage sales over the years than everyone else on the block put together. She didn't believe in book ownership, with all the good libraries around. Her father was a briefly famous architect, and she thought throw pillows ruined the lines of a couch. She knew about spring cleaning. She always said you couldn't carry extra baggage and be happy. After your father left to pursue an archeology degree in Greece and then took a vow of silence, she sold everything he wasn't smart enough to take with him, including gifts you had given him over the years—a pair of onyx cuff links, a mahogany wine rack, a brass change collector.

You are overwhelmed with dizziness, or a sudden realization: It is your mother's fault that you cling to everything you own, everyone you meet. She *made* you this way, with her executioner's skill in putting the past behind her. She doesn't respect you; how could she? You hoarded letters and old tests, worn-out sneakers and outgrown clothes, while she discarded bank branches, whole departments of customer-service specialists. Time to move on, she likes to say, whether she's talking about the next stop on a business trip or her failed marriage, but moving on is precisely what you would like to avoid because the future is unknowable, and therefore who could be sure whether you might need to use that [insert noun here] again. Best to hang on a little longer, just to be sure.

Temptation
     resistance to, 2.89

When it's dark and you're tipsy and feeling sorry for yourself, and you're counting your women friends who are married now and send Christmas cards with their babies on them and the men friends who are married and no longer keeping in touch with you anymore, and you know better than to measure your life against someone else's yet cannot stop yourself, do not approach any packed boxes because you might decide to keep all the old things that are crowding out the new and because like it or not, it is time to move on. Pack it up.

Gifts

from women (Macy's), 5.054
from men (Hallmark), 5.055

Late night, time for the knickknacks. Yes, this means the miniature porcelain puppy collection and the cluster of cookie tins. They will be challenging, so you were wise to save them for last. There's a certain rhythm in getting rid of your possessions; you have to work up to the keepsakes. Reward yourself if all goes well—even if it doesn't, then, just for trying. Perhaps this experience will help you understand your mother a little better, although you might need less legal substances for that kind of insight.

The miniature English spaniel the yachtsman gave you after the first time you had sex goes first into the London Gin box. Why is it you're getting rid of all the things men have given you? You scan your apartment, looking for things that women have given you. You realize, upon inspection, that your women friends give gifts you *use,* in your favorite colors, like scented stationery and bubble bath, and that this fact alone is a fine argument for lesbianism, which several of your relatives suspect you of, anyway. After all, you're a liberal, single, thirty-one-year-old woman. What more do they need to know?

Now for the series of small pastoral watercolors, all gifts

from the Silicon Valley programmer. Sigh loudly, but don't relent. Turn next to the pile of decorative boxes, each containing bent paper clips, cracked shells, dry perfume samples—dump these things that are the next step up from dust in the universe and stack the boxes neatly into old London Gin. It's almost full, and your dog, peeking around a yet unsorted pile of magazines, looks disoriented and needful of some fresh air. Time for a walk.

Dogs. *See also* **Companions, 8.11**
    brief arguments for, 9.21

When you get back, there's a message on your voice mail from the man who is smarter than you. He sounds so casual, so detached. How is your spring cleaning going? his recorded voice chirps. He doesn't sound the least bit miserable to be alone.

Or maybe, you think, maybe he isn't alone anymore. Press your hand against your forehead until you can choke down the desire to drive to his condo and catch him with some new, unsuspecting woman. Tell yourself you're on her side, whoever she is. Tell yourself you'd only bad-mouth him to help her. Don't return his call.

Your dog is sitting patiently at your feet, waiting for you to unclip his leash. Pet him for being so quietly supportive, so *there* for you. Let him lick your face. Feed him and watch him eat. It's so easy to please him. He will never edge toward the door at the end of the weekend, unsure of when he'll be back in town. He will never pretend to be happy without you.

Now. Look at all those full boxes lining your bedroom wall. You are doing so well. In fact, at this rate, you might have to pace yourself, just to have enough packing to get you through the night. Take your time; allow yourself to savor this slow emancipation from your pack-rat past. Screen your calls. Your progress might invite a false sense of strength, but you may not be ready to face the man who is smarter than you.

Men. *See also* **Companions, 8.11**
    as fine wine, 10.145
    as bad-luck clothes, 10.39

You are disappointed that he hasn't tried calling you again. Here it is, midnight; if *you* had called *him* three hours ago, you'd have already left several more messages, each one more desperate than the last. Don't linger on this thought; it is too depressing. Instead, focus on all the room you will have for new ideas, new experiences.

You are sitting on your living-room floor, spent, amber Jack Daniel's swirling in the bottle as you dangle it in lamplight, when there's the knock at your door. Don't even bother to check who it is; you know. There he is, leaning against the door frame, hair wet and sticking up from the shower, hands in the pockets of his impeccably faded jeans. You can't even breathe; you seem to feel his voice more than hear it when he asks you to come with him for some Mexican; he's in the mood for tacos, maybe a few margaritas. Slip on your sandals, splash some cold water on your face to no effect, and the next thing you know, you're in that restaurant he took you to on your first date.

He's talking about nothing in particular, and you're fuming. What was this weekend about anyway? Why did you bother? You should just go home and bury yourself in your boxed belongings. You haven't learned a thing. You snag a waiter by his vinyl chaps and order a margarita *grande. Ándale,* you tell him.

Two margaritas later, you are not sure if you should excuse yourself and vomit in the restroom or wait until you get home. Really, you're pathetic, but you feel pretty good. Or, more accurately, you feel nothing, and that's a welcome change.

As gracefully as you can, rise to your feet. You know there is nothing you can do about the past. Tell him you're ready to go. In the car, you are not so inebriated that you miss his sideways glances, the way he manages to brush your knee when he shifts gears. Resist it—you know he isn't good for you, and yet the thought of him free in the world, or worse, free and happy with some other woman, makes a pocket of acid bubble up in your throat. Close your eyes, tilt your head, let your hair fall away from your neck. You can afford these languid movements that he will mistake as invitations, you can arch your back in a stretch just as your dog can roll over and expose his soft belly to you—there is no danger, nothing to fear. This man, who may or may not be smarter than you, can't have you, in spite of what he may think, because tonight you will open your front door just wide enough for yourself. Enjoy this new feeling of power—it will not last when you are alone. Still, tonight, imagine your future, how good to yourself you might be the next time around. Imagine knowing what's right and sticking by it.

If only you could pack this man in a box along with everything else—what kind of box would you choose? A wine box, definitely, that had held something pricey and complicated. Imagine leading him gently to it—instead of to your bed—and folding him inside. This box, safely sealed, you could shove to the back of your closet, along with the bad-luck clothes you can't get rid of but are hoping to redeem. Maybe someday he will emerge, aged and wiser. And maybe you will even have room for him.

Printed in the United States
By Bookmasters